OH, NO . . . GOD, NO . . . HELP ME—

In absolute terror, Ryan flattened herself against the garage door. She could hear the footsteps now . . . dragging toward her across the floor . . . like something heavy . . . dead . . .

Like something inhuman.

"Marissa," Ryan whispered, and she began inching along the door, praying the thing couldn't hear her, wouldn't find her, the relentless blare of the horn filling her head, disorienting her in the terrible darkness—

"Marissa," she whispered again, "I didn't mean it . . . I tried to hang on—I—"

From the other side of the garage, Marissa's car started up.

"Help me," she murmured, and in that split instant she realized that something was near her— beside her in the dark—she could *feel* it—the darkness pulsating with its *presence,* its *danger*—

"Oh, God . . ." She put out her hand and felt heavy, wet fabric . . . damp human skin . . . icy cold . . .

Something slimy coiled around her neck . . .

Shrieking, Ryan's head snapped back and hit the wall, and through the pitch darkness she saw a soft explosion of stars . . .

Books by Richie Tankersley Cusick

FATAL SECRETS
VAMPIRE

Available from ARCHWAY Paperbacks

SCARECROW

Published by POCKET BOOKS

Most Archway Paperbacks are available at special quantity discounts for bulk purchases for sales promotions, premiums or fund raising. Special books or book excerpts can also be created to fit specific needs.

For details write the office of the Vice President of Special Markets, Pocket Books, 1230 Avenue of the Americas, New York, New York 10020.

T3034

RICHIE TANKERSLEY
CUSICK

AN ARCHWAY PAPERBACK
Published by POCKET BOOKS

New York   London   Toronto   Sydney   Tokyo   Singapore

This book is a work of fiction. Names, characters, places, and incidents are either the product of the author's imagination or are used fictitiously. Any resemblance to actual events or locales or persons, living or dead, is entirely coincidental.

AN ARCHWAY PAPERBACK *Original*

An Archway Paperback published by
POCKET BOOKS, a division of Simon & Schuster Inc.
1230 Avenue of the Americas, New York, NY 10020

Copyright © 1992 by Richie Tankersley Cusick

All rights reserved, including the right to reproduce
this book or portions thereof in any form whatsoever.
For information address Pocket Books, 1230 Avenue
of the Americas, New York, NY 10020

ISBN: 0-671-70957-7

First Archway Paperback printing January 1992

10 9 8 7 6 5 4 3 2 1

AN ARCHWAY PAPERBACK and colophon are
registered trademarks of Simon & Schuster Inc.

Cover art by Gerber Studio

Printed in the U.S.A.

IL 7+

for Mom and Dad
on your 50th anniversary
for all your love and faith

Prologue

"If I die out here in the cold, it'll be all your fault," Marissa snapped, burrowing deeper into her jacket. She glanced up at the sky and tugged impatiently on her necklace. "Look—it's snowing harder, and we're miles from anywhere. I could be home smelling the turkey bake, instead of out here in the woods with you, looking for stuff to make stupid garlands with and—what was that? Did you hear something?"

"Hear what?" Ryan McCauley frowned over at her older sister, then redirected her gaze to the softly piling drifts around them. In the darkening maze of gnarled trees, her voice sounded almost eerie. "What's the matter with you? You've been jumpy ever since you drove in from school last night."

Marissa carefully avoided Ryan's eyes. "The trip upset me, that's all. Some jerk stayed on my tail practically the whole way home."

"Oh, right. A half-hour drive, and you're nervous. Maybe you wouldn't be so nervous if you drove it a little more often and came home to see Mom. If Steve didn't teach there at the same college, we wouldn't even know you're alive. At least he sees you on campus once in a while."

Marissa pressed her lips together and ducked her head. Ryan had the distinct feeling that her sister was about to say something but changed her mind.

"Anyway, I thought you'd like coming along with me—we've never been all the way up here to North Woods before, and I thought it'd be fun to get out of the house awhile and do some exploring." She waited for a reply, but when none came, she sighed and turned away. "Come on . . . I need some more pinecones."

"Your boss said a *few*, didn't he? I'm sure he didn't mean to clean up the whole forest—hey, where are you going?" Marissa cast an uneasy glance behind them but followed as Ryan ducked beneath some tangled limbs and came out into a snow-covered clearing. "And it's just the perfect job for you, too, isn't it?" she muttered. "Working in a toyshop, for God's sake."

"It's not just a toyshop," Ryan said indignantly. "Mr. Partini is a dear, sweet man, and he makes practically all the toys himself."

"Then if he's so sweet, let *him* come out here and freeze *his* butt off—"

"Marissa, he's old! He can barely walk around as it is! We've been making store decorations for weeks now—Mr. Partini's even been working on them at night! You know how busy shopping will be tomorrow —the day after Thanksgiving! I told him to be sure and call me if he needed more greenery or anything, so—" Ryan broke off and stared at Marissa, whose eyes were fixed on the surrounding trees.

"Ryan . . . I know I heard something move—do you see anything?" Ryan followed her sister's gaze and tried to shake off a sudden chill that had nothing to do with the weather. "How could you see through all this snow anyway? It's probably just the wind. Or a deer or something."

"I want to leave, Ryan. I want to leave now." Marissa jerked one hand through her hair, red ribbons tangling in her long blond curls. "We need to drop that film off before the drugstore closes."

"Film?" Ryan stopped and brushed snow from her mittens, her face puzzled. "Did you give it to me already?"

"You put it in your purse!" Marissa's voice sharpened. "Ryan, I mean it. We have to get that film developed—"

"Okay, okay, just a few more branches, and then we'll go. And if we'd just split up, like Mom suggested in the first place, instead of you following me everywhere, we'd be done a whole lot faster! I don't know what your big fat hurry is anyway—they won't even pick the film up till tomorrow—"

"I told you—I have to get those pictures before I go back to school—Ryan, what was that?"

This time Ryan stood and looked where Marissa was pointing. Between the swirling snow and the fading light of late afternoon, the woods and shadows ran together in one ghostly blur. Marissa, poised statuelike, was clutching a tree trunk and trying to peer deeper into the gloom. Ryan walked up behind her and stopped. She listened for a long time, then finally gave an exasperated sigh.

"Marissa, I don't hear anything—what is—ouch!"

To her surprise, Marissa suddenly whirled and grabbed her by the shoulders, shaking her, staring wide into her eyes.

"Ryan," she said, her face grave, "if I tell you something, will you promise not to tell a soul? Not a single soul? You *swear?*"

"Well . . . yeah, I guess so—"

"Don't *guess* so!" Marissa's vehemence startled her. "Ryan, I'm not kidding around—*swear!*"

For a long moment Ryan looked back at her sister. She could feel her own heart racing, and there was a knot tightening in her stomach. "I swear," she whispered.

"I think I'm in trouble," Marissa said. "Serious trouble."

It took a few seconds to register. "What . . . kind of trouble?"

As Ryan watched, Marissa gazed off into the woods again, twisting her necklace distractedly. "It's a long story, and I don't want to go into all of it right now."

"Wait a minute. Is this something you should tell Mom—"

"No!" Marissa's voice raised, and she tightened her grip. "Especially not Mom! Not yet!"

"Okay, okay, don't get so upset—I won't tell her!" Ryan was growing more alarmed by the second, and she tried to pull away. "Marissa . . . you're really scaring me. What's *wrong?"*

"I'm not sure—not a hundred percent anyway—but I'm *pretty* sure." As Ryan squirmed free, Marissa put her hands to her head, then let them drop. She leaned back against a tree and closed her eyes.

"Sure about what?" Ryan stepped closer. "When will you know?"

"In a few days. Then I'll have to decide what to do. Oh, Ryan, it's just too complicated, I don't even know where to start!" For a minute Marissa looked as if she might cry. "I just never thought he'd do something like this—"

"Oh, God. Oh, God, Marissa, it's some guy, isn't it? What have you done now?" Ryan was fighting to stay calm, and she took another step closer. "I mean it, this better not be a joke—"

"I swear it's no joke!"

"Then who's *'he'?* Have you told him about your . . . problem?"

Marissa shook her head. "I think he might suspect something—but sooner or later I'll have to go to him with the truth—"

"Oh, Marissa . . ."

"That's why I had to talk to you—and why you have to *promise!* This *has* to be our secret till—oh, God, what was that?"

Ryan nearly jumped out of her skin as Marissa grabbed her again. "What is *wrong?* What are you—"

"Was that something moving? I thought I saw—"

"This *is* a joke, isn't it? You're just trying to scare me into leaving! I *hate* when you do stuff like this!" Angrily Ryan plowed into the woods again, only half conscious of Marissa's rapid breathing as her sister tried to keep up. "Okay—*I'm* going right over here up this hill—and *you* go straight ahead over there—see —there's another clearing way off through those trees —and finish getting the pinecones! I'll meet you back at the car!"

"Ryan—wait!"

"No!"

"You're such a brat, Ryan! Come back here!"

"No! I'm sick of your stupid games, Marissa! Now, just hurry up so we can go *home!*" She watched as Marissa threw her a hateful glare and flounced off into the woods.

Grumbling, Ryan turned and went in the opposite direction.

She was on her knees, digging holly from underneath a fallen log, when she heard Marissa's screams.

In the soft, white stillness the terrified sounds ripped through her heart, and Ryan dropped everything and began to run back.

"Marissa! Where are you?"

As the screams came again, Ryan crashed through the forest and fought her way through, shouting her sister's name. She could hear Marissa's cries growing closer—only now there was something else— something so horribly out of place in this picture-perfect countryside—

Water.

Churning . . . splashing . . . *water*.

"Oh, God—*Marissa!*"

As Ryan tore free of the trees, she saw the snowbank lying so deceptively just a few yards away, its surface broken, big chunks of ice upended, revealing a dark, jagged hole and black water beneath. And as Ryan spotted Marissa's head—Marissa's arms thrashing— she raced toward her sister in a haze of terror.

"Marissa!" she shrieked. "Hang on!"

"Ryan! Help me!" Marissa's cries gurgled as she went under, and as Ryan started across the snow, the ground suddenly began breaking up around her, splitting apart with a slow, steady groan—

Oh, my God—it's not a clearing at all—there's water everywhere—"No!" Ryan was on her stomach, sliding, crawling, and she could see Marissa's face again, Marissa's fingers, blue, blue, and the wide, frantic eyes, the arms reaching—

"—ian!" and it *sounded* like her own name, but Ryan couldn't be sure. *Ryan?—dying?—*

"I'm here, Marissa! I'm coming!"

"—ian!" But Marissa's head was underwater, and Ryan couldn't hear.

"—elp! *Help* me! My hand—*sleeve—*" And Ryan was trying to understand Marissa's shouts as the water choked them off again and again. With a sob she grabbed out for Marissa's sleeve and hung on with all her strength.

"I've got you! Come on—I've got—"

Marissa's arm jerked, nearly pulling Ryan into the water. She felt herself slip helplessly toward the edge of the hole. She looked down and saw Marissa's sleeve still in her grasp, part of Marissa's jacket, floating . . .

"No, Marissa—please—hang on—hang—"

The hole was empty.

"Oh, God, no—"

As Ryan watched in horror, she saw the smooth patch of snow-cleared ice, and beneath it, Marissa's face, eyes bulging, mouth gaping in a soundless scream.

And then . . . Marissa was gone.

Chapter 1

Three Weeks Later

There it was again—that feeling of being watched.

Ryan paused at the edge of the school parking lot, oblivious to the horde of students around her. As her heart raced uneasily, she glanced back at Fadiman High and squared her shoulders. "It's Christmastime," she mumbled to herself. "And no more bad things can happen, because it's my favorite time of year."

"There you go again," a familiar voice said with a sigh, so close behind her that she jumped.

"Oh, Phoebe, you scared me to death! I didn't hear you!"

"Didn't hear me?" Phoebe's mouth twitched, and she nodded at the jostling crowds around them. "You mean, standing here in the middle of a wild stampede, and you didn't hear me coming?" She smiled then, showing her dimples, but it quickly faded as she watched Ryan solemnly scanning the rows of cars, the laughing groups of kids. "Ryan . . . did you hear me? Hey, are you—"

"Fine," the other girl finished mechanically. The lot held only the usual faces and voices, and she flashed

Phoebe a look that was almost guilty. "For a minute—I don't know . . ."

"Someone following you again?" Phoebe giggled. "I keep telling you, it's probably just some guy trying to get up his nerve to ask you to the New Year's dance!"

"No . . . I don't think so. Oh, well, it's probably nothing. Just the season. You know how I get this time of year."

"Yeah, more like a little kid than usual," Phoebe responded fondly, falling into step beside her. "Believing in everything. Magic and wishes and Santa Claus and—"

"Well, why not? It's just as easy to believe as not to."

Phoebe studied her a moment, then added softly, "Even though this Christmas will be so . . . different?"

Again Ryan studied the leaden sky, her heart feeling suddenly as heavy. "You can say her name, Phoebe. I'd rather you say her name than just act like she never existed or something." She saw the flush on her friend's face and immediately took Phoebe's hand. "I'm sorry. It's just that . . . it still doesn't seem real that Marissa's dead. I keep thinking I see her every time I turn around. . . . I think I hear her calling me when I'm home. And people still stare at me—"

"You're imagining it," Phoebe broke in. "And even if they *are* looking, it's just because . . . you know . . . they're sorry."

"No. I know what they're thinking."

Phoebe took a deep breath and patted Ryan gently on the back. "Come on. You told me you weren't going to start all this again."

"I can't help it. I know when Mom looks at me, she's seeing Marissa and wishing things were all switched around—"

"Ryan . . . please don't keep doing this to yourself. I can't stand to see you so unhappy." Phoebe stopped and stared earnestly into her friend's face. "You've got to stop feeling responsible for what happened. There wasn't anything you could do—it was just a freaky thing."

"But I didn't save her." Ryan's eyes teared up. "And we'd been fighting—"

"Sisters fight all the time, Ryan, *please*—and you couldn't have known there was water underneath that snow—"

"If only we hadn't gone up there . . . if only she hadn't gone with me." Ryan closed her eyes, trying to shut out the regrets she'd gone over so many, many times before. She didn't feel Phoebe take her shoulders and give her a gentle shake.

"It wasn't anybody's fault," Phoebe insisted. "Think about it, Ryan, how many people you could blame for what happened that day. You told me yourself, Mr. Partini's still never gotten over it. And your mom's the one who made Marissa go with you. And poor Steve—he suggested you check out North Woods. And *I* had to help my mom, so *I* couldn't go with you. Maybe if I had, Marissa wouldn't have died.

Maybe if I'd gone, we *both* could have saved her. Do you blame *me* for what happened?"

"Of course not," Ryan said in a tight voice. "But I'm the one who left her. And one second I had ahold of her—and—then—" She raised haunted brown eyes to Phoebe's clear blue ones. "She was gone, Phoebe. She was trying so hard—and then she was just gone."

"Oh, Ryan"—Phoebe looked like she was going to cry herself—"it was just a horrible accident. It's awful, and it's tragic, but it *happened*, and it *wasn't your fault!*"

"If only I hadn't gotten mad at her—I was so mean—"

"Ryan, you couldn't be mean to anybody." Phoebe thought a moment, then gave Ryan her let's-be-logical look. "Think about me and Jinx! We're *always* at each other's throats, and I really *am* mean to him because I *like* to be, and *nothing* bad ever happens to him! Am I making sense?"

"No." Ryan stared at her a long moment and, in spite of herself, had to smile. "It's not the same. You'd be *glad* if something awful happened to Jinx."

"You're right. I would." As Phoebe pretended to wistfully consider the possibility, Ryan gave her a shove.

"You're terrible."

"I know I am. That's why I have you—to balance me out." Phoebe nodded, and then her face went serious again. "Ryan, you've got to get on with your own life. I swear I'm not trying to minimize what's happened, but you're going to make yourself crazy if you keep on like this."

Ryan sighed. "Come on, you can walk me to work." She did smile then, much to Phoebe's relief, and they headed away from school and started through town. "Remember that red shirt I got Marissa last Christmas? You and I got it at that discount store and it was on sale, and we thought it was so glamorous?"

Phoebe tilted back her head and laughed out loud. "And she wore it out that night without a coat, and it rained—"

"And it was her first date with that weird guy she'd been drooling over for so long—"

"And the blouse got all wet—"

"And the color ran out all over everything—"

"The poor guy thought she was bleeding to death—"

"And she was so mad at us, she wouldn't talk to us for weeks!"

They were roaring with laughter now, and it felt so good, washing over the deep, deep pain, soothing it away. Phoebe linked her arm through Ryan's and tugged her down the sidewalk.

"You get a tree yet?"

"No. I keep bringing it up, and Mom keeps ignoring me. All she does is drag herself to work, come home, and sit in Marissa's room. She still keeps the door closed . . . sometimes she even locks it. It's like a shrine or something."

"Tell Steve," Phoebe said helpfully.

"I guess I'll have to. He's the only one in her life these days."

"Ooh." Phoebe winced. "I know a nasty when I hear one."

"Well, it's true," Ryan said defensively. "And the thing about you is—"

"I'm so smart."

"You *think* you are," Ryan corrected, trying not to smile. "Just because you've known me since first grade—"

"And we were best friends from day one—"

"Doesn't give you the right—"

"To know you so well," Phoebe finished triumphantly. "Come on, Ryan, you might as well accept the fact that your mom's going to marry Steve someday—she's crazy about him! As a matter of fact, *I'm* crazy about him."

"You're crazy about every guy. In fact, you're just crazy."

Phoebe thought a moment, then nodded. "So I have a very healthy attitude about the opposite sex. Why couldn't Steve have just met me first?"

Ryan shook her head indulgently. "I thought you were all *for* him and Mom."

"I am! I think it's cute. And I think *he's* cute. That smile of his—and he's so funny—the way his hair's a little thin on top—and that mole on his—"

"God, Phoebe, what have you been doing, watching our house with binoculars?"

"I also like the fact that he has a sports car and a

14

boat and likes to treat you and me to dinner a lot. Face it—not every widow gets a second chance at love—and it's a good idea for your mom to think of financial security."

Ryan couldn't help chuckling. "You sound like a commercial. And the money must be in his family because I know college professors don't make that much."

"A college professor," Phoebe said dreamily. "He's so intelligent, too."

"Forget it, Phoebe, you'd make a terrible professor's wife." Ryan ducked her head as a cold blast of wind rushed at them along the sidewalk. "And anyway, he's going to interview for a department chairman's position at another university, so he might be moving away."

"No! You didn't tell me! When?"

"In a few days. Mom's already starting to mope."

"So if they *do* get married, maybe your mom'll have a brand-new start in a brand-new place." Phoebe looked pleased. "That's good for her. Now we just have to worry about you."

Ryan sighed. "Don't worry about me."

"You need a boyfriend," Phoebe said stubbornly.

"I don't want one."

"Yes, you do, and especially now. Steve and your mom are a twosome. And . . . well . . . you're not."

Ryan felt arguments welling up inside her, but as Phoebe held her in a steady gaze, she sighed again and gave in.

"Why are you doing this to me?"

"Because you need a *guy!* Ryan, you are the most giving, the most caring person in the whole world! Except to me, that is. It's just that you and your mom both lost someone you love, and now your mom's got Steve and you don't have anyone. Life's not fair, but that's the way it is." She nodded for emphasis, then cast Ryan a sly look. "I'm *still* in love with Steve, you understand, but I don't think life's fair."

"Well, if life were fair, Marissa wouldn't have died." *If life were fair, it would have been me who fell through the ice, not Marissa, and Mom would be happier and things would seem more normal and right. . . .*

"If life were fair, I wouldn't have Jinx. Little brothers would be against the law. Especially ones who are only a year younger." Phoebe rolled her eyes. "If life were fair, I'd be an only child. Or the trolls would have stolen him at birth."

"So what's Jinx done now?" Ryan asked, amused. Through all their growing-up years together, she couldn't remember a time when Jinx hadn't been a constant source of irritation to her friend.

"What's he *done?*" Phoebe echoed. "He hasn't done anything. He doesn't *have* to do anything except exist. He doesn't have to do *anything* except be his own obnoxious self. Isn't that bad enough?" She looked slightly incredulous. "Can you believe girls actually *call* him? He gets phone calls all the *time* at home. Carla Smith called—and she's a senior! Girls think he's cute! *And*"—she paused for effect—"I have my suspicions that he's got his heart set on Tiffany Taylor! Seriously!"

Ryan chuckled. "You're kidding—that little sophomore cheerleader who walks like this and giggles all the time? I thought she was interested in what's-his-name—that nerdy guy in Jinx's class—"

"That's what I heard, too—the junior class vice president. Wow. Tiffany and Jinx—can you even imagine? Or that anyone in her right mind would think Jinx is *cute!*"

"Well . . ." Ryan said generously, "he *can* be kind of cute when he wants to be. With that baby face of his."

"Yeah, when he thinks he's in trouble, or when he wants something. You can have him. I'll give him to you. For free! If life were really fair, you'd take him."

"And if I had a dollar for every single time you've threatened to give him to me—"

"See?" Phoebe shot her an accusing look. "You don't want him, either! If life were *really* fair, my parents would lock him up someplace and throw away the key. And . . . I'd have naturally curly hair." She laughed, looking pleased with herself as Ryan regarded her in disbelief.

"You are so impossible! I'd give *anything* to have hair like yours. Look at this—brown hair, brown eyes—*dull!* If life were fair, I'd be blond. And I'd have a million dollars."

"Well . . . you're rich in friendship. You have me!"

"Oooh . . . bad."

Phoebe laughed and started to hug her, then suddenly shook her arm. "Look over there—on that corner by the bus stop—isn't that Winchester Stone?"

As Ryan followed Phoebe's stare, she felt a strange flutter go through her chest, and she quickly ducked her head. "Yes, that's him. Come on, don't look, let's just keep walking."

"He is the most *gorgeous* guy I have ever seen—"

"Come on, Phoebe, quit looking at him. Just hurry up—"

"I mean it, Ryan, he is *so* sexy. And to think your sister actually went out with him."

"You know she only did it so all her friends would be jealous. She used him. After a couple dates she lost interest."

"Oh," Phoebe moaned, "I wish he hadn't graduated last year—maybe I'd have had a chance, now that we're finally seniors."

"From what I hear, he doesn't have a girlfriend," Ryan said casually. "Why don't you get Jinx to fix you up? He's always down at the garage."

"Oh, him and his creepy little friends—and Winchester's teaching them all to work on cars— God!" Phoebe made a fist and beat on her forehead. "Working with Winchester practically every day! Can you imagine being that close to Winchester *every day!*"

Ryan toyed with the thought, then pushed it firmly away. "What does Jinx say about him?"

"Nothing. *Nobody* knows anything about Winchester. You never see him with friends . . . you never see him with girls—not that every female I've ever talked to wouldn't sell her *soul* to go out with him! You have to admit he's gorgeous. You *have* to have noticed—"

"Well, of course I've noticed. He used to come by for Marissa—how could I help but notice?"

"Ha! And I bet you were hiding, I bet you never even came down to talk to him in person!"

"Well"—Ryan shrugged, her voice defensive—"he *did* come to see Marissa, after all. He didn't come to see me."

"Oh, Ryan, it's no wonder you never have a date. They're all afraid they'll give you a heart attack if they come near you!" Phoebe groaned in frustration. "Look at him. He has that shy look, but he's always in those tight jeans—"

"Phoebe, honestly!" Ryan shook her head, then shot a hasty glance back at the figure on the corner. "He's kind of a loner, I guess. Maybe he doesn't like having friends."

"Doesn't he ever come around to see you? To talk to your mom or anything?"

"No, why should he? I told you Marissa didn't care about him."

Phoebe couldn't resist looking back at the bus stop one more time. "Well, I still think it's strange, that a guy that great looking should be alone so much." She sighed, falling into step with Ryan once more. "I'd love to just talk to him. Just be alone with him and"—she shivered—"oh, I bet he's a great kisser. And other things—"

"Phoebe, will you quit looking at him!" Ryan tugged on the other girl's arm, and Phoebe immediately tripped over the curb. "You don't want him noticing us, but you keep looking back at him. Just stop it and try to walk like a normal person!"

At some unspoken signal, the girls began to run, not stopping again until they had turned a corner onto a dingy side street. As they slowed down and tried to catch their breath, Phoebe grinned and pointed to the brightly lit store window several feet ahead of them.

"Well, here we are! Cold weather and Christmas coming and this great job waiting for you! What more could you ask for?"

"A best friend with half a brain." Ryan grinned back. "An A on my history test tomorrow."

"Oh, darn, I forgot about that stupid test!"

"I *have* to make a good grade. I'm really doing awful in my classes."

Phoebe looked concerned. "But I thought the teachers were being really understanding."

"They are, but they can only be *so* understanding. I feel like I'm really losing it . . . I can't concentrate . . . I can't study . . . I don't hear things in class . . . sometimes I come to and realize time's passed, and it's like I've just blanked out."

"Give yourself time," Phoebe said. "It's only been a few weeks, and you've been through a lot. The teachers know that. Hey—I'll be by later to study, okay?"

"Okay. I'll make sure there's plenty of popcorn."

They paused on the sidewalk in front of a shabby brick building, smiling as they peered through the frost on the front window. Beyond a quaint sign reading PARTINI'S TOYSHOP, a Santa Claus doll supervised his workshop. In caps and aprons, amidst pots and wood shavings and sleepy-eyed reindeer, mechanical elves measured and cut, hammered and sawed, assembling toys while Christmas carols sang out from a hidden speaker. Ryan felt a rush of emotions go through her—an ache for her childhood, an emptiness for Marissa—and she gave Phoebe a playful shove to keep the tears from coming.

"See you tonight. Thanks for the escort."

"You're not still walking all the way home from here, are you?" Phoebe's eyes went worriedly back and forth across the little alleyway, and she frowned. "I never have liked this place after dark, way back here by itself."

"What do you mean?" Ryan teased. "This is the artsy section of town. This is where us creative types work."

"Well, it just doesn't seem safe to me," Phoebe grumbled. "And it's getting dark so early now."

"It's better than waiting for Mom to come and get me. She always forgets anyway. Look—it's safe." Ryan steered Phoebe back to the curb, pointing out more rundown shopfronts. "See? The art gallery? The bakery? The used bookstore? The Coffeehouse? All these antique shops?" Her voice sounded confident, but as she suddenly remembered her strange feeling back at school, a shiver went through her. "And Mr. Partini wouldn't let anything happen to me." She smiled now, thinking of the toy shop owner and the friendship they'd developed over the past six months she'd been employed.

"This place is creepy enough, but you still have to walk out on that old road," Phoebe said stubbornly.

"I've walked that old road hundreds of times. Since I was old enough to walk home from school."

"Well, I still don't like it. Just please be careful, okay?"

"I promise. See you later."

Ryan waved until Phoebe had disappeared, and as she finally stepped through the door, the fragrant warmth of the shop enveloped her like a welcoming hug.

It had started as a temporary job, a way to make extra money, but even after all these months, Ryan still hadn't grown tired of the toy shop. It wasn't like any other place she'd ever known, with its dark musty corners and cobwebbed ceiling, its dusty shelves and creaking, uneven floorboards. What had at one time been a showroom for antique furniture had become through the years a hopelessly cluttered wonderland of handmade toys, with Mr. Partini's workshop at the back. Tiny locomotives trundled through the rooms on ledges along the walls. There were dolls of all sizes and kites shaped like animals; tins and tops and windup toys. From shadowy corners carousel horses watched with painted eyes that seemed to move. There was even a magnificent dollhouse with a backyard pond where the dollhouse family enjoyed seasonal outings. Ryan loved them all, and now as she sniffed the fresh evergreen from the decorated Christmas tree, she felt all her concerns melting away.

"Mr. Partini!" she called. "Mr. Partini, it's me!"

Of course he'd be at his workbench, and of course he'd pretend he hadn't heard her so he could act surprised when she poked her head through the curtain at the rear of the store. It was a game they always played, and as Ryan shrugged out of her coat, she began to pick her way carefully through the maze of toys and furniture.

And then she felt it again.

That strange tingly sensation of eyes boring into her back.

She had told Mr. Partini time and again how easy it was to overlook customers in the hopeless disarray, and now, as she slowly turned, her eyes swept each corner, expecting to find some customer browsing half hidden in the gloom.

"Hello?" Ryan called. "Is anyone there?"

No answer. As her eyes continued around the shop, she suddenly noticed a movement from the front window.

It was hard to see the figure clearly from its place out on the sidewalk; all Ryan could make out was a lumpy coat, a black ski mask with holes for eyes, and a cap pulled low on the head. One of the train whistles screeched, startling her, and when she looked again, the window was empty.

"You *are* a mess," she scolded herself and continued on to the back. As she entered the work area, she saw the toymaker's empty stool, where he should have been sitting, and uneasily she took down her apron from its hook on the wall. From behind her the bell tinkled over the front door, and she hurriedly walked out into the shop.

"Merry Christmas! If I can help you find anything, please—"

The cheery greeting died on her lips.

The shop was empty.

Funny . . . I could have sworn I heard that bell. . . .

Frowning, Ryan let her gaze wander once more over each crowded, shadowy corner, but when she didn't hear anything else unusual, she sighed and got to work.

"Okay, family, everybody out—the maid's here to dust!"

Ryan leaned in at the back of the dollhouse, where all the rooms lay open to view, but though she peered into the parlor, where the family should have been, it was deserted.

"It's no use hiding," Ryan joked, "I see *everything!*" But as she took a quick survey of all the other rooms, she stepped back, puzzled. *I know I left them in the parlor . . . maybe some kid moved them . . . maybe some kid stole them. . . .* She moved to one rear corner of the house and suddenly spotted the little dolls in their backyard, apparently enjoying some winter game as they clustered around the glass-mirror pond. "So there you are! What is this—a skating party and I wasn't—"

Ryan froze, her eyes riveted on the artificial water. From somewhere far away she heard screams . . . screams for help . . . but the room was deathly silent.

The mirror was broken, shiny shards of glass in scattered silvery pieces, and trapped there, far out from shore, was one of the dolls.

Only her head was visible . . . and her arms, reaching for help . . .

And the bright red ribbon that streamed from her hair onto the soft white cotton snow.

Chapter 2

Mr. Partini!"

As Ryan stumbled backward, a display of wooden blocks clattered down around her, and she screamed and ran for the back room.

"Mr. Partini! Where are you!"

"Yes, yes, *Bambalina!* I hear you! The whole street —it hears you, too, eh?"

To Ryan's relief, the back door opened and a bushy white head poked through, faded blue eyes twinkling behind round spectacles.

"What you so excited about, *Bambalina?* You just see Santa Claus? And he promised to bring you a nice young man for Christmas?" The heavy Italian accent gave way to a chuckle, but as Mr. Partini closed the door behind him, he finally focused in on Ryan's pale face. "What happened to you? Why you look so scared?"

"The . . . the dollhouse!" Ryan tried to steady herself with a deep breath. "The pond—it's broken—"

"What?" Mr. Partini lifted his head and made a disgusted sound in his throat. "You mean somebody busted up the mirror? Seven years' bad luck!"

"But the doll—you've got to come—"

"Yes, Ryan, I come—ah! There go my tools on the floor—clumsy me! Yes, yes, just let me pick them up. . . ."

Ryan could hear herself babbling as she flung the tools back onto his table, as she grabbed his arm and pulled him into the front. "She's drowning—in the pond—in the ice—" She could see confusion all over Mr. Partini's face, and as she got to the dollhouse, she gestured wildly. "See? The pond—"

"Yes, yes, I see the pond." Mr. Partini's head nodded rapidly up and down. "Yes, yes, but nobody drowning."

"Look—there—" Ryan's words choked in her throat, and she stared at the broken pond in the miniature backyard. The mirror still lay in slivers, but the doll was gone. Stunned, she leaned in close to the dollhouse. The family was back in the parlor. The drowning doll sat in a chair and wore no ribbon.

"No," Ryan murmured, stepping back again. "No . . . you don't understand . . ."

"Then you tell me, eh?" The old man shuffled forward, his kindly, wrinkled face full of concern. "You tell me, *Bambalina,* so I understand."

Ryan shook her head slowly. "She was in the pond."

"And you move her back inside?"

"No. I didn't move her."

"But . . ." Mr. Partini spread his hands, his face completely baffled. "How can that be? These no walking dolls—are sitting dolls!"

"But she *was* there," Ryan insisted, her voice

beginning to tremble. "She was in the pond, and no one would help her—"

"Ahhh . . . what you say to me, *Bambalina?*" He looked earnestly into her face, his confusion growing. "What—you think she need help, this little doll? Maybe she wanna go outside in the snow, eh? Yes, yes, is okay!" He nodded, pleased that he'd figured it out. "You help her! Put her outside! Whatever you want!"

"No . . . I . . ." Ryan's voice faded, and she bowed her head. "It . . . made me think of my sister."

She hadn't wanted to say it, but she couldn't help it. And now, seeing the look on Mr. Partini's face, she hated herself.

"Ah . . . Ryan . . ." His hand fluttered over her head, settled shakily on her hair. "Is much too sad. My worst heartache . . ."

"I'm sorry," Ryan whispered. "I didn't mean to bring it up." She watched the old man sink down onto a wooden trunk, and she sat on the floor beside him.

"Is very hard, losing someone." Mr. Partini sighed. "Like my Rosa . . . twenty-five years now . . . but I never forget."

A long silence drifted by. Mr. Partini closed his eyes and rocked gently, lost in thought. After a while he spoke again.

"I say to myself, is a good idea to put fresh things, green things in the toyshop. Nice for customers . . . nice for you and me . . ." He shook his head sadly. "No. Was bad idea."

"No, Mr. Partini, it wasn't a bad idea. It didn't have anything to do with what happened." She smiled wryly, hearing Phoebe's own words coming out of her mouth. *Why is it always easier to comfort everyone else instead of me?*

"Twenty-five years," Mr. Partini murmured. "My Rosa . . . my love . . ."

"Mr. Partini"—Ryan nudged him gently, and he looked at her as if he'd forgotten where he was—"Mr. Partini, *someone* broke that mirror."

"Aah . . . not your fault," he said kindly, patting her cheek with one blue-veined hand. "I no blame you—you not worry, eh?" He got up and gathered the broken pieces of the mirror, shuffled over, and dropped them into a wastebasket. "No more worry. Everything okay now. I get a new mirror. Everybody happy."

"Someone moved the doll, Mr. Partini," Ryan said, trying her best to be patient. "Between the time I found it and you came in. Someone must have been here, and I didn't know it—"

"You have other things on your mind." Mr. Partini patted her shoulder, smiling. "Crazy things up here sometimes, just like me!" He tapped one finger to his forehead, his smile spreading, lighting up his whole face. "Is normal, eh? I hear voices—they say, 'Work harder, Guido Partini, you way too slow, even for an old man!'" He laughed heartily, catching Ryan in a hug. "You okay, *Bambalina.* You go home now. Rest. Come back tomorrow . . . feel better, eh?"

"I shouldn't leave, Mr. Partini. I'm here to work—"

"Yes, yes, and all these customers need help!" He flapped his arms at the empty room and tried to look serious. "Go away, all of you! My little friend here needs to go home, and I can only wait on fifty of you at one time!"

In spite of everything Ryan began to feel better. "Well, I hope all the customers don't start looking like that weird one in the window."

Mr. Partini turned and stared at his front window display, then back to Ryan, his expression more blank than ever.

"You make a joke with me." He shrugged his shoulders good-naturedly. "But I don't get it!"

"No joke, Mr. Partini." Ryan couldn't help smiling. "He was out on the sidewalk in a big fat coat with his face all covered up."

"I no see this big fat guy." Mr. Partini shook his head. "Maybe he fat with money, eh? Maybe he come in sometime and buy all my toys for his fat babies!"

Shaking her head in amusement, Ryan followed him back to the workshop and got out of her apron.

"Where were you when I got here?"

"Is a funny thing! I hear knock on door. I say, who's there?" Ryan chuckled as the old man counted out the events on his fingers. "Voice say 'Delivery.' I say 'I no expect delivery.' Voice say 'Delivery.' I go out, eh? Nobody there. Nobody in whole alley." He stared at Ryan, dismissing the whole incident with a wave of his hand. "So maybe another joke on me. Bad boys playing around."

Ryan considered it, nodding. "Well . . . I suppose it could have been a joke. . . ."

"Or maybe shop is haunted!" Mr. Partini slapped

his leg and gave a laugh. "They break mirror—they call me outside! Those bad, bad toys, eh? Causing trouble!" He laughed again, ushering her to the front door, then regarded her thoughtfully as she put on her coat. "You bundle up warm, *Bambalina*—no catch cold in the snow." Gently he reached out and patted her cheek, then closed the door after her as she went outside.

It was nearly dark. Ryan usually enjoyed the shorter days of winter, but now it looked ominous outside, and she was thankful for the dim light from the other shops.

That doll . . . reaching for help . . .

A raw wind gusted out from an alleyway, twisting old newspapers around Ryan's ankles. Catching her breath, she tore them away, then watched them scatter out into the street.

The doll . . . with the red ribbon . . .

"It was my fault," Ryan whispered now, walking faster, head bent against the wind, "my fault that you're dead, Marissa—"

An earsplitting squeal made her look up in alarm— she saw the headlights only inches away and felt a crushing jolt as she spun backward and sprawled facedown onto the curb.

"Hey, are you okay?"

Stunned, Ryan lay there on the pavement and gave in to the strong hands that took her shoulders and gently eased her over.

"Are you hurt? Say something—can you talk?"

As Ryan gazed up into the young man's face, she

felt her breath catch in her throat. Winchester Stone was staring down at her, silhouetted against the slate-gray twilight.

"Can you hear me? Can you move?"

At long last Ryan found her voice, though it came out little more than a croak. "I . . . I think so."

"Try, then. Move your arms."

Ryan gingerly did so, relieved when nothing seemed to be broken.

"Now your legs."

Again she did as she was told. She could feel his arm beneath her shoulders, propping her up. His other hand moved to her right ankle, and then to her left, carefully testing for broken bones. Flustered, she struggled to sit up.

"I'm fine. Really. I just need to get up now."

"You sure?"

"Yes. I'm really okay. Just . . . surprised."

"Surprised." As he echoed her words in his soft, slow voice, Ryan could see the fear on his face relaxing a little. "Surprised," he said again. "You stepped out right in front of me—I didn't even have time to honk the horn. You're lucky I didn't kill you."

Ryan got clumsily to her feet, avoiding his eyes. He picked up her things and handed them to her.

"I'm sorry," she said. "I've just had my mind on other things lately."

His glance was quick and curious. His eyes shifted back to the street.

"Forget it," he said quietly.

"I'm . . . I'm Ryan McCauley," she stammered.

"I know."

"You do?" She bit her lip, embarrassed, and tried to be casual about brushing herself off.

"I went out with your sister," he said, and his eyes swung back to her again. "But I never saw you at your house."

Because Phoebe was right, I was always hiding upstairs.

Ryan shrugged and tried to smile. "Well, I was— you know, around somewhere probably."

Without warning Winchester turned back to his truck, but stopped after only a few steps. He kept his back to her, one hand resting on his hip.

"I'm sorry about her," he said.

Ryan stared at his tall, lean frame, his thick black mane of hair hanging just below the collar of his denim jacket.

"You helped look for her. I never thanked you."

There was a long silence.

"I guess . . . you haven't heard anything," he said at last. He sounded uncomfortable, and Ryan shook her head, forgetting that he couldn't see her.

"They still haven't found her body. They told us they might never find her. . . . I hate to think that."

"It's the river," he said quietly. "The current's so strong . . ." He turned around and looked at her, but his face was in shadow. "Do you need a ride some-where?"

"I'm going home," she said, then added quickly, "but really, I'm used to the walk."

"It's dark. That's a pretty long way to go." He

moved to his truck and opened the passenger door. "Get in."

She felt that curious fluttering in her chest again and glanced back in the direction of the toyshop. *Maybe I only thought the doll was in the pond . . . like when I blank out at school and then realize half the class is over. . . .*

"—the door?"

"What?" Ryan's mind snapped back, and she saw Winchester staring in her window.

"I need to close your door."

"Oh, yes—yes—sorry."

She watched as he slammed the door and climbed in the other side. The pickup was old and battered, and it was all she could manage, not to bounce off the seat at every bump. She tried to study Winchester from the corner of her eye and sensed great calm and strength behind his handsome features. When he suddenly turned off the main road to her house, she realized that somehow she'd missed the whole trip.

"Well . . . thanks a lot." Ryan pushed on the door handle, but it wouldn't budge. She pushed again. "I really appreciate the ride—" She was shaking the handle now, and nothing was happening, and he was just sitting there staring at her while she made a total fool of herself. "It really was nice of you—"

"You have to unlock it," Winchester said. To Ryan's embarrassment, he reached across her, pulled up on the lock, and shoved the door open.

"I-I—thanks," Ryan murmured. She scrambled out and headed straight across the yard to the front door. As she reached the porch, she couldn't resist one last backward glance. Winchester was leaning out his window watching her, and as she bolted inside, she heard the truck's engine fading down the road.

"Mom?" she called. "You home?"

"Up here," came the toneless answer, and Ryan's heart sank. When she looked in Marissa's room, Mrs. McCauley was sitting listlessly on the edge of the bed.

"Come on, Mom," Ryan coaxed. "Let's go downstairs, and I'll make hot chocolate."

"I missed her today," Mrs. McCauley murmured. "Even more than usual." When Ryan didn't answer, she roused a little, her eyes searching for Marissa's clock. "Are you home already? It must be late—"

"No, I'm early." Ryan peeled off her coat, relieved when her mother finally faced her.

"Are you sick?"

"Sort of. Not really."

Her mother nodded and turned away. "That's so like you, Ryan. Can't you decide? So different from your sister. . . ."

Ryan sat down but couldn't bring herself to touch her mother's shoulder. "Maybe I'm trying to catch the flu. It's going around school."

Mrs. McCauley held a thin hand to Ryan's forehead. "No fever. Maybe you're just tired. I've told you a hundred times, you shouldn't stay up so late to study."

I stay up late because I can't sleep, and when you see my grades, you'll find out that all the studying hasn't helped. "I know—let's go out for dinner."

"I can't, Ryan. Steve flies in tonight, and I promised to pick him up."

"God, Mom, he has his own boat, can't he even afford a taxi?" The words were out before she could stop them, and her mother's face grew even more remote. "I'm sorry." Ryan reached for her mother's arm . . . hesitated . . . drew her hand away. "That was a rotten thing to say."

"Yes, it was. Especially since Steve thinks so much of you."

"Well, anyway"—Ryan sighed—"I forgot Phoebe's coming by later to study and—" She broke off, following her mother's gaze to the windowsill, where a smiling photo of Marissa stared back. "Mom?"

"When I'm in here," Mrs. McCauley murmured, "it's like it used to be. I can feel her . . . she's alive."

Ryan's eyes swept the room, and she suppressed a shiver. Nothing in the room had been changed or removed or rearranged since the day of Marissa's death. Ryan didn't like the strange feeling the room gave her. She only came in here when she had to drag her mother out into the world of the living.

"Just like today," her mother went on. "Like today when I just started missing her so much, I thought I couldn't bear it. I thought, my beautiful daughter is dead, and the pain is more than I can stand—"

"Mom . . . please . . ." *You still have me . . . doesn't that help . . . even a little?*

Her mother's eyes swung reluctantly back to Ryan's face, and an ironic smile quivered at the corners of her mouth. "I know I'm being silly. Everyone's told me it's impossible she could have survived. Maybe . . . with the spring thaw—"

"Mom—"

"It's just that I keep thinking of her, lost out there somewhere, and all alone, and wondering why we haven't found her and brought her home. . . ."

Ryan was shaking. She made it to the hallway and stood there looking back.

"I know I'm being morbid," Mrs. McCauley went on, her voice breaking, the tears coming, yet still she stared at Marissa's photograph, still her eyes never moved. "Morbid and completely illogical, but maybe she really *did* survive somehow, maybe she's sick somewhere and confused and someone's taking care of her and she can't remember who she is or what happened. Maybe it'll suddenly come back to her, and we'll hear a knock at the door and—"

The doorbell pealed through the silent house, and Ryan jumped as her mother turned frightened eyes toward the hall.

"It's probably Phoebe." Ryan backed gratefully toward the stairs. "Mom? Did you hear me? I'm going now."

Hurrying down, Ryan breathed deeply, trying to rid herself of the stale stench of Marissa's room. The porch light was on, and through the frosted glass at the top of the door, she could make out an indistinct form, someone standing there, head lowered.

"Phoebe, you silly," Ryan scolded, jerking open the door. "What'd you do, forget your key again—"

But it wasn't Phoebe standing there on the porch,

arms heaped with gaily wrapped packages. As Ryan stared, the young man looked up, his wide, full mouth relaxing in a polite smile, the presents shifting slightly as he stepped forward.

"Is this the McCauley residence?"

"Yes," Ryan mumbled. In the glow of the light she saw dark blond hair brushed back from a high forehead, and narrowed blue eyes that swept over her without so much as a blink.

"I'm delivering these presents. From Marissa."

Ryan knew she was staring, but she couldn't help it. In the sudden quiet her voice sounded unnaturally loud. "From . . . I'm afraid there must be a mistake—"

"No mistake," he interrupted, stepping closer, the smile fixed on his lips. "I know Marissa's dead."

"You . . . then . . ."

"You must be Ryan," he said, and in that instant she saw something flicker behind his eyes, something tighten in his smile.

"Yes. Yes, I am."

He bent his head, his chin deep in the collar of his jacket. His voice sounded muffled, but Ryan could still hear each word.

"You're the one who let her drown."

Chapter 3

Ryan had a strange feeling of being suspended in time. She saw the smile on the stranger's face, and she heard footsteps descending the stairs behind her, but she couldn't seem to make herself move or speak.

"Ryan?" It was her mother's voice, fearful, on the staircase, and as Ryan mentally shook herself, her mother spoke again. "It isn't Marissa, is it? Tell me it's—"

"Charles Eastman." The young man peered around Ryan, his smile open and friendly as Mrs. McCauley hovered at Ryan's back.

For a moment Mrs. McCauley looked as confused as Ryan felt. "I'm . . . I'm afraid I don't—"

"I was a friend of Marissa's," he said quietly. "A very good friend."

"Marissa?" Mrs. McCauley echoed, and the longing in her voice stirred Ryan at last. "You knew Marissa?"

"We had classes together. We'd been going out awhile."

"Charles . . . Charles . . ." Ryan could see her mother struggling to think back, to place him somewhere in Marissa's interrupted life. "I'm sorry, I . . ."

"You mean Marissa never mentioned me?" He chuckled. "Isn't that just like her—with her string of boyfriends, I'm not surprised. But that's okay." He smiled understandingly. "There's no reason you should know me. Actually, I've been wanting to come and see you for a long time—ever since I heard about . . ." His voice trailed away, and his face went serious. "Well, I was cleaning out some stuff last week, and I found these." He held the packages out and took a step closer. "We used to go antique hunting together, and I guess some of her things got mixed up with mine. I knew she meant to give these to you for Christmas." His voice softened, his eyes suddenly sad. "Anyway, I wrapped them and decided to bring them myself. I know it's what she would have wanted."

Throughout his whole speech, Ryan had been watching, listening, feeling as if she were invisible. *"You're the one who let her drown."* He *had* said that, hadn't he, as she'd stood there holding the door? Yet the charming young man before her now *couldn't* have said those horrible words—and through a slowly clearing fog, Ryan heard her mother's voice taking control at last.

"Come in, Charles, come in—Ryan, don't leave him freezing out there on the porch! Close the door."

Ryan felt him move past her into the hall. She closed the door and watched as her mother led Charles into the living room and gestured to a chair.

"Ryan, take the packages and his coat. You can stay

for a while, can't you, Charles? Wouldn't you like something hot to drink? Coffee? Tea?"

"Coffee'd be great, but only if it's already made." He smiled at Ryan and draped his coat across her arm. She hadn't remembered following them into the room.

I'm scaring myself. First I was seeing things that weren't there . . . and now I'm hearing things that nobody said. . . .

"Ryan!" Mom's voice, firm. "The coffee?"

She felt herself nod and was glad to escape to the kitchen, glad to be doing something she didn't have to think about. *Pot . . . filter . . . coffee . . .* Her hands moved slowly, but her mind was racing. *"You're the one who let her drown."*

He didn't really say that. He couldn't have.

Ryan slipped back to the hallway, positioning herself so she could watch Charles without being seen. He was sitting forward in his chair, hands clasped together on his knees, his expression intense as if determined not to miss anything her mother might say. From time to time he slowly flexed his fingers, reminding Ryan of a contented cat. She moved closer, propping herself in the doorway, and was surprised when Charles turned and gave her a winning smile.

"I wish you'd sit down. I didn't want you to go to any trouble on my account."

"It's no trouble," Mrs. McCauley assured him and gestured toward Ryan. "I'm so sorry, Charles, I didn't even introduce—"

"Oh, I'd know Ryan anywhere," Charles broke in smoothly. "From the way Marissa described her. She talked about you a lot, Ryan. You must have been so close."

He was staring at her intently. Something about his expression seemed almost mocking, but Mrs. McCauley didn't seem to notice.

"Marissa's—accident—has been pretty hard on Ryan. She was with Marissa when it happened, you see—"

"So I heard," Charles said softly. His eyes brushed over Ryan, leaving a peculiar coldness in their wake. "I'm sure it's something . . . she'll never forget."

You did say it . . . when I opened the door, you said what I thought you did—"I'm going to Phoebe's," Ryan burst out, and she could see the disapproval on her mother's face as Mrs. McCauley motioned toward the kitchen.

"Ryan, I wish you wouldn't run off. I thought Phoebe was coming here to study. Isn't that coffee ready yet?"

"I forgot. She *was* coming here, but we decided to go there, instead. I just forgot."

"Ryan's always forgetting things." Mrs. McCauley gave Charles a strained smile. "Not like Marissa. Marissa never had trouble making up her mind—"

"It doesn't look very Christmasy in here," Charles broke in pleasantly. "You decorate about as much as I do."

"Oh, we *used* to decorate . . . I just . . ." Mrs.

McCauley's eyes flicked to the mantel, more photos of Marissa, more painful reminders. "It just didn't seem right somehow. . . ."

To Ryan's surprise, Charles said, "But what about Ryan? It must be hard on her, your not going ahead with family traditions. If it were me"—his eyes slid to Ryan's puzzled face and then shifted away—"I guess I'd feel like I was being . . . you know . . . punished."

Ryan stared at him, but he kept his gaze averted. "I'm going to Phoebe's," she said again, but her mother didn't seem to hear.

"I suppose you're looking forward to Christmas," Mrs. McCauley said to Charles. "Being home from college, spending time with your family—"

"Actually, I'm not." Charles shook his head politely. "My parents are divorced. My dad's in Europe on business, and my mom's remarried, living out on the West Coast. I've been hanging out at school, but it's so dead around there, I decided to just get in my car and drive."

"And you don't have friends to stay with anywhere?"

"No, I'm heading out again in the morning." He laughed softly. "I booked myself a room at that motel outside of town."

"But that's a terrible place to stay! There aren't even any decent restaurants nearby!"

"Really?" Charles looked surprised. "Marissa's the one who gave me the name of that place—in case I ever got here over the holidays."

"Did she?" Mrs. McCauley leaned forward, her face wistful and sad. "Tell me how you knew her. What you remember about her."

Charles's voice was barely a whisper. "I really miss her."

"Oh, I do, too. More than anyone can understand—"

"Goodbye," Ryan broke in. "I'm going." But nobody seemed to care, and she escaped out the kitchen door.

What kind of a creep had Marissa met up with this time! Ryan thrust her hands in her jacket and trudged off across the yard, down the slope behind the house. It was a shortcut she often took to Phoebe's, one that ran through fields and woods instead of along the main road into town. The air was nippy, but she welcomed the sting of it against her cheeks. She couldn't have stood another minute in the same room with Charles Eastman.

It was a good twenty minutes' walk to the Evanses' house at the south edge of town. As Ryan wiped her feet on the welcome mat, she noticed both cars gone from the driveway, but she could hear loud music blaring from upstairs, which meant Jinx was home.

"Phoebe!"

The music kept going, and Ryan shouted again as she climbed the stairs to Phoebe's room.

"Phoebe, it's me! Let's study here tonight, okay?"

"Go home, McCauley, who invited you?"

As Ryan neared the landing, Jinx suddenly appeared in the upstairs hall, lounging lazily against the railing. There was something about Jinx that always made her smile, even though she and Phoebe usually felt like strangling him, and she hid a smile now as he purposely blocked her way to Phoebe's room. He was a year younger, but every bit as tall as she was, and Ryan guessed that if he ever decided to unfold his body from its perpetual slouch, he'd be even taller. She and Phoebe had come to the conclusion long ago that Jinx had been born in tattered jeans and dirty sneakers—trading off seasonally between holey T-shirts and stained sweatshirts. The jeans he wore tonight had a torn back pocket and rips in both knees, and his hair, as usual, looked like he'd just gotten up and forgotten to comb it. His quick brown eyes never missed a thing, though most of the time they looked deceptively bored.

Ryan stared at his ear and frowned. "So that's where Phoebe's earring went. She'll really kill you this time."

"Like I'm worried." His thin body slouched itself forward over the banister.

"And new laces in your shoes. Fuchsia. How sweet."

"Yeah. I thought so." A slow, disarming grin crept across his face, showing the one dimple in his cheek, the only similarity to Phoebe. Ryan wondered how he could often look so cuddly and be such a holy terror.

"Don't tell me she's not here."

"She's not here."

"But we were supposed to study—"

"Forget that. Some guy called, and she went out."

"Really?" Ryan brightened. "Was it Michael Kilmer? Did he finally ask her to the dance?"

Jinx shrugged. "Her eyes glazed over. That's all I know."

Ryan sighed. "Well, I wish she'd at least called me."

"She did call you. She called you lots of things. But I stuck up for you."

"I meant on the phone. You know what I meant—"

"She left a message with your mom."

"Well, that explains it." Ryan grimaced. "Do you know when she'll be back?"

"What do I look like—a secretary?" He snorted and started back down the hall to his room. "I got things to do."

"Important, I'm sure." Ryan heard the thump of a basketball hitting the wall, and she trailed along, following the sound. Jinx's room was a perfect reflection of his personality, and she paused in the doorway, shaking her head.

"How can you live in here? Where's your bed?"

Totally unbothered, Jinx yanked his headphones down over his ears and promptly flopped down amidst pillows, tangled covers, books, dirty clothes, car magazines, cassettes, and baseball cards. "Don't you have something to do?" he yelled. "Besides standing around adoring me, I mean?"

Ryan sighed and went down to the kitchen, stopping to admire the Christmas tree along the way. She'd always loved the Evanses' house—its cozy atmosphere always encouraged warm visits and heart-to-heart talks. Helping herself to a ham sandwich, she sat down and opened her history book. *I have to study . . . I have to concentrate.* But every time she closed her eyes to memorize something, Charles Eastman's face popped into her mind and spoke to her. *"You're the one who let her drown."*

"I didn't," Ryan whispered, pressing her hands over her eyes. "I didn't let Marissa drown. You didn't say that . . . why did you say that?"

A sudden noise made her jump. Jinx was propped in the doorway staring at her.

"There's a guy at my house," Ryan said stupidly.

"So what'd you do, kidnap him?" Jinx sauntered in, opened the pantry, shrugged, left the door open. "You're gonna have to think up new ways to get a date, McCauley."

"I'm serious."

Jinx stood at the sink with his back to her. After a moment he glanced over his shoulder.

"What guy?"

"He just showed up. Just tonight, out of the blue. With Christmas presents he said Marissa'd bought for us. He was at school with her. I guess they went out."

"So?"

"So . . . I think he's weird."

"You should know." Jinx turned his attention back to the countertop. He took an apple from a bowl and bit into it with a loud, intentional crunch.

"I shouldn't have gone off like that," Ryan mumbled. "I shouldn't have left Mom there alone with him. I shouldn't even be here." She stared down at her book and frowned. "I should go. I don't know why I even came here in the first place."

"Well, when you finish this fascinating conversation with yourself, let me know what one of you decides to do."

"Maybe I should call the police." Ryan sat straighter, her frown deepening. "Do you think I should call the police? I mean, we don't know anything about this guy—do we?"

Jinx shrugged. "I give up. Do we?"

"Then maybe I *should* call the police—"

"No, no"—Jinx reached toward the phone—"let *me* call them. They have places for people like you who go around arguing with themselves."

Ryan closed her eyes for a moment. When she opened them again, Jinx was staring at her curiously.

"Hey, McCauley . . . you okay?"

"He said I let Marissa drown," Ryan murmured.

"What?" Jinx's face hovered between skepticism and surprise, and he took another bite of apple, continuing to talk around it. "That's dumb. He didn't say that. Why'd you think he said that?"

"Because . . ." Ryan's mind went back . . . the front door opening . . . Charles Eastman's face peering over the packages . . . "I just did. That's what it sounded like."

"That's really dumb," Jinx said again. "Tell me how he said it. How you *thought* he said it."

"'You're . . .'" Ryan took a deep breath. "'You're the one . . . who let her drown.' That's how it was."

"Your mom heard him say it?"

"No, she wasn't there. She came down right after."

"Then you must have gotten it all messed up in your head." Jinx looked annoyed now, and he spit some seeds into the sink. "He probably said, 'I'm new in town' . . . or . . . or maybe 'I'll hang around.' Something like that."

"No, I don't think so."

"You don't *think*—that's the whole problem with you," Jinx snorted. "I mean, why would a total stranger ring your doorbell and say something dumb like that? Hey—where you going?"

"Home." Ryan gathered her things and paused by the front door to put on her coat. "Tell Phoebe to call me the minute she gets home. Okay? No matter how late."

"Yeah, yeah." Jinx waved impatiently, following her onto the porch. "Man, it is *cold* out here . . . and you *walked* over? What a loony."

"Mom needed the car to pick up Steve. Anyway, it's not that bad."

"Anyway, like I'd trust your judgment." He shivered and thrust his hands into his jeans pockets. "How come you never drive Marissa's car?"

"You know why," Ryan retorted. "It's part of the shrine. Sacred. Can't be touched."

"So touch it. What's your mom gonna do?"

Ryan considered a moment. "Cry. Mope. Sulk."

"Ah. The usual."

"I hate it there, Jinx. It's like a funeral home. I want a Christmas tree."

"So *get* a Christmas tree."

"I want to be happy again."

"Then stop making yourself unhappy. Only you can."

She looked at him in mild surprise, and he shrugged his shoulders with a lopsided grin.

"See you around, McCauley. Don't talk to strangers —or yourself—on the way home."

Ryan stood there a moment after Jinx had gone inside. She watched the Christmas tree glowing in the front window . . . she breathed in the sweet aroma of winter and woodsmoke and pine trees that lined the drive. The air felt heavy and wet with the promise of snow, and she walked quickly, slowing down only when she reached the frozen creek near her house.

Stopping, Ryan felt the hair prickle along her scalp. The woods were full of silence, and then the cold, cold sigh of the wind.

Ryan frowned, her hands making fists in her pockets.

She listened, and the night listened back.

She started walking again, her ears straining through the deep winter night. She thought she heard a rustle of leaves . . . the soft sucking of mud. A raccoon, she tried to tell herself, or maybe a deer . . . Annoyed with herself, she started to duck under a fence.

It's back . . . something . . . watching me . . .

With a gasp Ryan spun around, challenging the empty fields with wide, frightened eyes. *No, I'm only imagining it, just like the doll in the pond, just like*

Charles's speech at the door, just like I've started imagining lots of things since Marissa died—yet she began to run, across the fields, up the last slope to the house, her breath ragged in her throat as she fell into the kitchen, as she sagged against the door—

"Mom! Mom, where are you?"

But of course Mom wasn't there, Ryan remembered now, she'd gone after Steve and they'd eat out afterward and *thank God I'm home safe, and Charles is gone*—

Ryan felt weak as she dragged herself upstairs. She left the switch on in the hall, and she left her door open, and then she turned on every lamp in her room, flooding herself with bright, safe light. She took hold of the sweater she was wearing and began pulling it up over her head.

"I'd close the door if I were you."

Gasping, Ryan whirled around, her arms tangling in her sweater as she tried to jerk it back down again.

Charles Eastman was standing in her doorway.

Smiling.

"I knocked, but I guess you didn't hear me," he said. "Sorry about that."

Ryan stared at him and felt her cheeks burn as his eyes moved from her sweater to her face. "What are you doing here? What are you doing in my house?" She took a step toward the phone on the nightstand by her bed. "Get out of here right now."

"But didn't you know?" And his mouth fell open in mock surprise. "Your mom asked me to stay."

"She . . . what!"

"She invited me to stay. To spend Christmas. I was just going to the motel to get my stuff."

Ryan saw the smile widen across his lips and the way he took another casual step into her room. She heard her own voice, and it sounded strange and hollow.

"But . . . she couldn't have. We don't even know you."

"Your mom likes me." He smiled again and came closer, hesitating at the foot of the bed. "And Marissa liked me," he said softly. He leaned toward her.

His smile was gone.

"But *you* don't like me. Do you, Ryan."

As Ryan stared back at him, she saw Charles lift his hand . . . felt his fingertips trace lightly down one side of her face . . . across her shoulder . . . down her arm . . .

"Well, who knows?" He shrugged, and again something flickered behind his smile, behind his eyes, that made Ryan's skin turn cold. "I just might surprise you."

Chapter 4

"**H**ow could you?" Ryan demanded before her mother could get in the back door. "I can't believe this!"

Mrs. McCauley dropped her purse on the counter but didn't turn around right away. "Ryan, I don't think I need to explain myself to you—I'm still the head of this house—"

"Welcome home, Steve!" Steve said with forced brightness behind her. "Gosh, Steve, it sure wasn't the same with you gone! Come on, ladies, it's too late for an argument tonight, okay?"

"Steve, do something!" Ryan looked at him as he poured himself a cup of coffee and sat down at the table. "Can't you make her listen?"

"It's not his decision to make," Mrs. McCauley said. "I *want* Charles to stay—and Ryan, keep your voice down, I don't want him to hear you."

"He won't. He went to get his things."

"Have a nice trip, Steve?" Steve nodded in answer to his own question. "Hey, I sure did! And thanks for asking!"

"You don't even know him!" Ryan went on. "You don't know anything about him! He could be—"

"He and Marissa were good friends," Mrs. McCauley said softly. She braced herself against the counter, her hands trembling. "If Marissa cared about him, then he's welcome here."

"Did you ever hear her mention him?" Ryan persisted. "Did you ever hear his name around here a single time?"

"I'm sure there were lots of friends we never heard about. You know how popular Marissa was."

"Leslie, I think what Ryan's trying to say," Steve began, clearing his throat, "I mean, she's really got a valid point, I think—"

"I want him here," Mrs. McCauley said, her voice beginning to quiver. "He was a part of Marissa's life. I want him here."

"Oh, Mom!"

"We don't have Marissa this Christmas, and Charles doesn't have his family. The least we can do is share our holidays with him. For Marissa's sake."

Ryan stared at Steve, who silently mouthed a warning to let the subject drop. Ryan ignored him.

"*What* holidays? A couple hours ago you couldn't have cared less whether Christmas came or not. Now all of a sudden—" She broke off as her mother's shoulders began to shake, as the quiet sobbing filled the silent kitchen. Steve got up and motioned Ryan away, and she slipped dejectedly up to her room.

I don't even belong here. I'm an outcast in my own house. As Ryan stretched out across her bed, the telephone rang, and she was relieved to hear Phoebe's giggle on the other end of the line.

"Ryan—I'm in love."

"Again?" Ryan sighed. "Phoebe, something terrible—"

"Michael Kilmer called tonight and—you'll never guess—he asked me to the dance! He's been working up his nerve all this *time!* He thought I was going with *Randy*—I can't believe it—Michael Kilmer! I nearly fainted! No—no—I nearly died!"

"Was that before or after your eyes glazed over?" Ryan shook her head indulgently. "Phoebe, listen—"

"We went to the Coffeehouse and talked and talked —do you think I talked too much? I hate that, Ryan, I always worry—"

"Phoebe—"

"Anyway, a bunch of kids are getting together tomorrow night to go caroling, and I said you'd come—"

"Will you listen? I have to tell you—"

"We'll meet in front of school at seven. Then we'll go back to Michael's afterward for a party—"

"Phoebe—"

"—and I bet when you're there, someone'll ask you to the dance—"

"Stop—"

"I put the word out that you're still available—and I'm so sorry about studying tonight, but I really *did* try to call and—"

"Wait—I have—"

"Mom's giving me the evil eye. She needs to use the phone, so I have to go, okay? See you tomorrow— bye!"

Ryan heard the click and stared at the dead receiver in her hand. Slowly she replaced it on the stand, then sat up as a knock sounded at the door.

"What is it?"

Steve's head poked in, his smile cautious. "Truce?"

"I'm not upset with you. Come on in."

Steve nodded and closed the door behind him, leaning back against it as he surveyed Ryan sitting cross-legged on her bed.

"I know, I know," he said at last. "She's being weird again."

"You can't let her do this," Ryan said flatly. "It's totally insane, and you're the only one she'll listen to."

"Okay, I'll try. But she seems to have her mind—*and* her heart—set on this. Ryan . . ." Steve grew quiet for a moment, pursed his lips, looked at the ceiling. "Your mom's going through a really bad time right now—which isn't to say you're not, too"—his smile was sympathetic—"only she's not thinking about anyone but herself. It's not so unusual, you know, these crazy things she's doing. She's reacting to her grief and trying to work it all out in her mind."

"So we'll all get our throats slashed in the process," Ryan said gloomily. "While she's working out her grief, I mean."

Steve looked surprised, then laughed. "Boy, you really *don't* like Charles, do you? What's with all the hostility? You just met the guy."

"Nothing. I don't know." Ryan flopped down on

her stomach and propped her chin in her hands. "Okay. I know that look. What'd I say?"

A chuckle sounded low in Steve's throat, and he shook his head, giving in to a grin. "You're too much, Ryan."

"Don't give me that. You're wondering something. Out with it."

"Okay, then. I'm wondering why you're down on this poor guy. I know I haven't met him yet, but I have to trust your mother's judgment, at least a little! We don't have any reason to doubt he's a friend of Marissa's, and you're already accusing him of throat-slashing! Do you know something about him maybe the rest of us don't know?"

"How could I know anything about him?" *Except he accused me of killing my sister.* "Marissa never mentioned him. What about you? Haven't you ever had him in one of your classes or something?"

"Come on, Ryan, the campus is bigger than this whole town! I don't know *everybody*. Though he does seem kind of familiar."

"So is he telling the truth or not?"

"Well"—Steve shrugged—"his story sounds believable enough to me. And since this isn't my house, I can't very well throw him out if your mom wants him here."

"That's the trouble. She doesn't know what she wants," Ryan said irritably. "I don't trust him. He's too . . ." She spread her arms in frustration. "Too nice to Mom."

"Thanks," Steve said, deadpan. "Not like me, who's a real jerk, huh? Thanks a lot, Ryan."

"I didn't mean that. You *are* nice to Mom," Ryan said quickly as Steve laughed.

"Tell you what. The least we can do is find out if he's really going to school where he says he is."

"How will you do that?"

"Look through my directory. And if he's not there, call the admissions office."

"But will they tell you? Is that confidential or something?"

Steve shook his head. "The only problem will be finding someone in the office over the holidays."

"You won't forget, will you?" Ryan was relieved when he smiled.

"Not if it'll make you feel better. Just let's not talk about this in front of your mom, okay? I don't want to upset her any more."

Ryan sighed. "Just don't tell me I have to be nice to him." She put a hand to her forehead as the doorbell rang. "That's probably him now. We better not let Mom catch us talking."

"Right." Steve opened the door and peered cautiously out into the hall. He gave Ryan a thumbs-up sign and left.

I really am going to flunk that history test tomorrow. Once more Ryan opened her textbook, but before she could tackle her notes again, another knock sounded on her door. This time it was Mrs. McCauley who looked in, and Ryan could tell from the expression on her mother's face that she wasn't going to like whatever was about to happen.

"Ryan, I want you to let Charles have your room."

"What!"

"He's going to be here for a few days, at least, and—"

"At least! Mom, are you—"

"And I can't put him on the couch. If it were for a night, that'd be different, but he'll need some privacy."

"What about me?" Ryan sat up, her voice thin and tight. "It's *my* room—I don't see why I have to give it up for—"

"You can sleep in Marissa's room," Mrs. McCauley said quickly, and Ryan stared at her as she rushed on. "It makes perfect sense to do things this way, and you'll be just across the—"

"Why don't you put *him* in Marissa's room? He was *her* friend!"

"No!" Mrs. McCauley burst out. She put her hand on the wall to steady herself, and Ryan could see her fingers clenching. "I don't want some stranger sleeping in there, do you hear me? I don't want some stranger in Marissa's bedroom—"

"But it's okay for some stranger to be in *my* room." Ryan looked at her accusingly. "It's okay for some stranger to be in our house."

"Hey," a voice in the doorway startled them both. Charles was standing there, a regretful smile on his face. "Hey, look, the last thing I want is to cause problems. I think it'd be best for all of us if I just leave."

"You can't!" Mrs. McCauley caught him by the shoulders, recovered herself, then pretended to straighten his collar. "No, Charles, please"—her eyes swung to Ryan . . . pleading—"I want you to stay. We all do. Don't we, Ryan?"

For an endless moment Ryan locked eyes with her mother. Then she looked at Charles. His expression was politely unreadable, yet somehow she sensed cunning watchfulness just below the surface. Very slowly she closed her book and got up.

"I'll move my things," she said. *But I won't stay in Marissa's room, I'll pack a suitcase and go over to Phoebe's, and I'll live there till this creep is out of our house. . . .*

But deep inside she knew she wouldn't.

She could never go off and leave her mother alone with him.

Chapter 5

So he's really staying in your room?" Phoebe's mouth opened in disbelief, and she leaned against her locker, blue eyes wide. "And you slept in Marissa's room last night?"

"No." Ryan sighed. She put one hand to her mouth to stifle a yawn, then rubbed her forehead. "I slept on the couch. I watched TV and studied till I fell asleep."

"Oooh." Phoebe gave a shiver. "I don't blame you. I'd feel really creepy sleeping in there . . . you know . . . where she used to be. So what else about this guy? What's his name—Charlie?"

"Charles. Eastman. And that's all I know about him—*nothing*. Oh, Phoebe, what am I going to do?"

"Well, what does Steve think about it?"

"He's going to try and find out if Charles really went to school with Marissa. Steve doesn't like the idea of him being with us, either"—Ryan shrugged—"but what can he do? He can't *force* Mom to listen. She's really determined about this."

"What's he look like? Charles, I mean. Is he cute?"

"You'd probably think he is." Ryan sighed again

and shot her friend a look. "Don't get any ideas, Phoebe, okay?"

"Well, he does sound intriguing." Phoebe grinned. She pulled some books from her locker and slammed the door. "I think you're way too paranoid. Let's just analyze it. Maybe this is a sign. Maybe you're looking at it all wrong."

"Whatever you mean, I don't think I'm going to like it." Ryan looked suspicious as Phoebe locked arms with her and maneuvered along the crowded hallways. "I know that gleam in your eye, and it usually means trouble for me."

"Okay, just listen." Phoebe talked fast, knowing they were already late for class. "There's no reason that I can see for you to be nervous. Charles *has* to be a friend of Marissa's. What other possible reason could he have for wanting to bring presents and stay with you for the holidays? I think it's really sweet that he liked Marissa so much, he'd want to get to know her family better. He's probably thinking it will help somehow, if he's there to cheer up your Christmas."

Ryan frowned, still skeptical. "Well . . ."

"And it's a real compliment to you and your mom that he'd feel so comfortable, he'd even want to stay."

"But he's not the same to me as he is to Mom," Ryan argued.

"How?"

They paused outside their classroom door. Ryan could see Miss Potter inside glancing from the clock to the bundle of papers in her hands.

"I . . . I don't know how to explain it. He's just different."

"Are you sure you're not imagining things?"

"Phoebe—he practically accused me of killing Marissa!"

"Oh, Ryan, honestly, you *must* have heard him wrong! What a horrible thing to say!" Phoebe almost laughed. "I mean, why would someone come on a mission of mercy and say something so outrageous? It just doesn't make sense! I'm *sure* you misunderstood him—like you've been getting your assignments wrong all week. You're not listening very well these days. You said so yourself."

Ryan saw Miss Potter's frown deepen as she gestured for them to hurry. Phoebe took Ryan's arm and shook it.

"It's a *sign,* Ryan. Charles Eastman came into your life to take you to the New Year's dance."

As Ryan gaped at her, Phoebe turned and hurried to her desk, leaving Ryan to trail behind.

"So glad you could spare some time for us, ladies," Miss Potter greeted them. And as Ryan slid miserably into her seat, she could already see the big fat F slashed across the top of her history test.

"Mr. Partini!" Ryan paused in the workshop doorway, relieved when the toymaker grinned up at her from his bench.

"Ah! You sneak up on me, *Bambalina!* You feel better, eh?" He held up a grinning marionette, squint-

ing at it from behind his spectacles. "This customer—
he wants it *delivered!* Today! So now Guido Partini is a
taxi again!"

"You've got to stop making all those deliveries for
people," Ryan scolded him lovingly. "They have just
as much time in their day as you have. It wouldn't
hurt them one bit to get themselves over here and save
you some trouble!"

"Ah, no, *Bambalina,* no trouble!" Mr. Partini
shook his head, catching his glasses as they slid down
his nose. "Is a little thing for me. I help them out, eh?
No bother!"

"Then let me do it for you. I'd like to."

"You do plenty. Too much sometimes. I no deserve
you."

"And you're too nice." Ryan tried to frown but felt
the corners of her mouth turning up. "If I've told you
once, I've told you a hundred times. You've got to quit
being so nice!"

"Then I be mean to you!" He tried to put on his
fiercest expression, but his twinkling eyes gave him
away. "I be mean to the toys! I tear down the
dollhouse! We punish those bad dolls for giving you
such a scare!"

Ryan laughed and went out into the shop. The
afternoon went quickly, with a steady flow of customers to keep her busy, and she was totally absorbed in
demonstrating a jack-in-the-box when Mr. Partini
politely excused himself and took her aside.

"I go now to deliver the puppet, *Bambalina.* You
can watch the shop, eh? Lock up when you go home?"

"I think I can handle that," Ryan teased. "But I still wish you wouldn't go running all over town. You look tired."

"Ah, is such a little thing," he protested, waving her back to her customer. "Just a little way to say thank you for buying my toys, eh? I see you in the morning!" Laughing delightedly, Mr. Partini went out the back door, leaving Ryan to tend the shop alone.

She was exhausted when six o'clock came. Her lack of sleep the night before was catching up with her, and the last customer was a picky, rude woman who couldn't make up her mind. As Ryan's eyes went impatiently to the window, she suddenly stiffened and gripped the counter with both hands.

She saw the lumpy coat and the black ski mask. She couldn't see the eyes, but she knew they were looking at her, could *feel* them as if they were only inches away.

"—please?" The woman stepped between Ryan and the window, waving a doll under Ryan's nose. Startled, Ryan jumped back.

"Excuse me?" She was craning her neck, trying to see around her customer, but the woman kept side-stepping, blocking Ryan's view.

"Too expensive." As the woman turned to leave, Ryan saw that the window was empty.

"Wait!" she called, hurrying around the counter, but the woman stomped out the door. Ryan stood for a moment peering out at the street. Unsettled, she put her hand on the latch to lock it, but a shadow suddenly filled the doorway, and she screamed as the door burst open.

"God, McCauley!" Jinx stood there, looking just as startled. "What'd you do—see your own reflection?"

"Come in here!" Ryan yanked him out of the way so she could lock the door. She glanced outside again, but the street was empty. "We're closed, Jinx. Go home. No! Stay here."

"I love a girl who knows her own mind."

"Did you see that man a minute ago?" Ryan looked again, half expecting the strange figure to materialize at the window.

"What man?"

"Big coat. Ski mask. At the window."

"Yeah. He robbed the place next door and took off." Ryan gave him a withering look. "I'm serious."

"You're seriously demented. No, I didn't see anyone. Why?"

"He was there yesterday, too. Just looking."

"Uh-oh," Jinx said gravely. "A compulsive window-shopper. Quick! I'll call nine-one-one—"

"No, you jerk, he was watching *me.*"

"Even worse. The guy is desperate beyond hope."

"Don't you have someone else to bother?" Ryan headed for the back room, sighing as Jinx followed.

"I have to get Phoebe something for Christmas," he announced.

"Well, that's nice of you for a change."

"Yeah, Dad's making me."

"If you really want to make her happy, why don't you move out?"

"Suffering gives her character." Jinx grinned. "Dad said there was something here she wanted."

"That teddy bear over there." Ryan began turning off lights in the back room. "I was going to get it for her, but you can if you want."

"Why does she want this dumb thing anyway?" Jinx picked it up and studied it, frowning. "How much?"

"There's a price tag on it. I thought you finally learned how to read last year."

"Kind of touchy tonight, aren't you?" Jinx gave a slow grin. "Couldn't be that new guy, could it? Got your fantasies working overtime?"

Ryan bristled. "The only fantasy I have of Charles is him getting in his car and leaving."

"Right. After the New Year's dance, you mean."

"I mean now. The sooner the better. I can't stand the guy."

"That's not what Phoebe said."

"Phoebe's too wrapped up in Michael Kilmer to know *what* she's saying." Ryan gave a last look around the shop. "Are you buying that or not?"

"Yeah, okay. You don't have to bite my head off." Jinx sauntered over to the counter as Ryan rang up the sale. "Can you wrap it for me?"

"Now?"

"Well . . . sometime before Christmas."

Ryan made a point of sighing loudly. "Just leave it here, and I'll wrap it tomorrow when I come in."

"Could you hide it, too? She might find it at home."

"Jinx, *no* one could find it if you hid it in your bedroom."

"Okay, then, if she's not surprised, it'll be *your* fault—"

"Well, she spends as much time at *my* house as she does *yours!*" Ryan slammed the drawer into the register. "Okay"—she sighed again—"I'll put it somewhere." She pushed past him to the door and stood staring out. "Oh, great—"

"What?"

"It's snowing."

"I coulda told you that. I thought you liked snow."

"I do. I just don't feel like walking home in it right now."

"Come on . . ." Now Jinx sighed loudly. "I'll give you a ride."

"In *your* car? The last time I saw your car, it looked like your room. There's probably something contagious in there."

"Relax." Jinx grinned and reached above her, holding open the door just wide enough for her to squeeze through. "You're so ugly, nothing in my car would jump on you anyway."

He managed to sidestep Ryan's fist, keeping his distance as they started down the sidewalk. Huge wet flakes fell lazily from the darkened sky, and as Jinx brushed them from his hair, Ryan stretched out one hand to catch a few on her mitten.

"Phoebe's wrong about Charles," she said again.

Jinx had a ready retort, but her troubled expression stopped him. "You're still all hung up about what you thought he said to you. About Marissa, right?"

Ryan nodded, falling into step beside him. They walked slowly, and she turned her face up, loving the feel of snow on her cheeks.

"To tell you the truth, I'm not even sure now if he really said it or not. I keep thinking what you told me—"

"Me? What *did* I tell you? Something wise, I'm sure."

Ryan nodded absently. "Well, why *would* he have said something so awful to me? It's such a . . . *cruel* thing to do." She thought a minute, glancing up at him. "He really is nice to Mom. Sweet and polite. It's so weird . . . part of me wants to think he's just a nice guy. And part of me keeps having this feeling he's up to something."

"Yeah? Like what?"

"That's just it, I don't know."

Jinx nodded amicably. "So what's your plan?"

"What plan?"

"To get this guy out of your house."

"I don't have a plan." Ryan made a face. "Mom wants him to stay, so I guess he's staying."

"Well, don't blow this, McCauley. If you're really nice to this guy, maybe you'll end up at the dance after all."

Ryan threw him an exasperated look. "And has it ever occurred to you that maybe I don't even *want* to go to the dance?"

"Yeah." Jinx gave a solemn nod. "Girls always say that when they haven't been asked."

Ryan tapped her foot impatiently as he opened her car door. "And I suppose you've got girls *begging* you to take them?"

"As a matter of fact—" Jinx began, but Ryan slid in and slammed the door. After going around to the other side, he climbed in and fixed her with a smug look. "As a matter of fact—"

"You can't fool me," Ryan said primly. "No girl in the whole school would be desperate enough to go out with you or your goofy friends."

"You're just jealous." He stuck the key in the ignition and gave it a turn. "'Cause I'm popular, and you're not."

"Popular?" Ryan stared at him. "Excuse me, Jinx, I thought you said *popular.*"

Jinx managed to keep a straight face as he stared back at her. "Mystique, McCauley. It's called 'mystique,' what I have."

"It's called 'mistake,' what you have," Ryan corrected. "And besides, I hear little Tiffany Taylor has her eye on the junior class vice president."

"So who cares about Tiffany Taylor anyway?" Jinx snorted.

"You do. So maybe I should talk to her, huh? And tell her what you're *really* like—all the little things about you that I've known for years and years. . . ."

This time she got to him, as she knew she would.

"You know your problem, McCauley? You're still mad 'cause I pulled your stupid doll's head off when you were six years old."

"And you're still brain-damaged 'cause Phoebe and

I held you down and tickled you till you cried and told your mom." Ryan chuckled as he tried to ignore her. "I bet Tiffany would like to know about *that*. I bet she'd think it's cute—"

"Cut it out, McCauley, you're not—"

"Does she know how ticklish you *still* are? Maybe I should tell her *that*, hmmm?"

"Come on, now, quit fooling a—"

Too late Jinx tried to defend himself, but Ryan cornered him up against his door and mercilessly attacked his ribs.

"Cut it *out*, McCauley—I'm stronger than you—"

"Not when you're laughing, you're not—and—uh-oh—look at this—you're *blushing*—"

"I am *not!* Come on, Ryan, stop it!"

"So much for mystique." Ryan laughed as Jinx finally managed to grab her hands and shove her away. As he fumbled to put the car in gear, she settled back against the seat, enjoying his efforts to regain his dignity.

"No more favors for you," he scowled, cool and in control again. "You're too dangerous to ride with."

"Your face is still red."

"Shut up."

By the time they reached the house, Jinx still wasn't speaking to her, but Ryan finally coaxed a grudging wave from him as she ran up to the door. The house stood dark and silent against the wintry sky, and as Ryan let herself inside, she wondered where everyone had gone. Marissa's room seemed even spookier as she paused in the doorway, as if every personal possession were waiting for its owner's return. Ryan crossed to the window and looked out, resting her forehead on the cold, smooth glass. She took a deep breath and closed her eyes.

From somewhere outside came the honking of a car horn—not intermittently, but constant—as if someone was leaning on it and not letting up.

Jinx? Has he forgotten something and come back? Puzzled, Ryan scanned the yard below and the drive along the house. There were no cars that she could see, yet the honking continued, setting her nerves on edge. Irritated, she hurried downstairs and out onto the front porch, halting in dismay.

The front yard was deserted. There were no cars near the house or in the driveway leading to the road.

Ryan rubbed a chill from her arms and went back to the kitchen. *Maybe I just missed it, maybe it was driving around back when I looked from upstairs—*

After grabbing a flashlight, she stood nervously out on the back stoop and put shaking hands to her ears. She could still hear the monotonous honking—on and on—*but there's nobody here, I can hear it, but there's absolutely nobody here—* Slowly she followed the driveway behind the house, and as she quickened her pace, she suddenly *knew* where the sound was coming from.

The garage. *And it's coming from Marissa's car.*

With numb fingers Ryan scrabbled at the latch, then heaved the heavy door upward. In the darkness she could just barely see Marissa's car along the far wall, and as she groped for the light cord which hung from the ceiling, she felt her heart turn to ice.

Is that someone bent over in the front seat? Leaning facedown on the steering wheel . . .

Ryan found the cord at last and gave it a jerk.

Nothing happened.

She yanked it again—again—but still the garage lay in darkness.

Like a statue, she stood rooted to the spot, her heart pounding, the sound of the horn going on and on, shrieking through her, every nerve ready to explode. She found the switch on the flashlight . . . felt her feet stumbling forward . . . saw the car getting closer . . . Her eyes slowly adjusted to the gloom, and she tried to make out the shape on the front seat of Marissa's car. . . .

The beam of her flashlight skittered over the windshield, casting pale, eerie shadows into the black interior. . . .

She saw the stiff upholstery . . . the dust on the dashboard . . . and it looks like a coffin, Ryan thought wildly, *a gray-lined coffin all musty and stale and sealed tightly away. . . .*

And then she saw the body.

Through a haze of disbelief, Ryan aimed the flashlight onto the driver's side and saw the human figure slumped forward . . . the head propped on the steering wheel, its face hidden . . .

The long blond hair streaming over its back . . .

Wet hair—

And the red, red ribbons tangled in the matted curls—

Ryan tried to scream, but no sound came out. The weak beam of the flashlight began to tremble violently, crazy shadows in a macabre dance over the slumped body in Marissa's car—

The body began to move.

Horrified, Ryan saw the shoulders pull slowly back . . . the head begin to lift sluggishly from the wheel—

"No!"

Springing back, Ryan heard the flashlight hit the floor, saw the crazy spin of light and shadow as it rolled under the car. As she whirled around, the garage door crashed to the ground, leaving her in total darkness. Sobbing, she stumbled forward, running her hands frantically over the door, mindless of the splinters and cuts as she searched desperately for the latch. As her fingers closed over it at last, she gave a shove but nothing happened. Slamming her shoulder against it, she moaned and staggered sideways.

The car door squeaked slowly . . . slowly open.

Oh, no . . . God, no . . . help me—

In absolute terror Ryan flattened herself against the garage door. She could hear the footsteps now . . . dragging toward her across the floor . . . like something heavy . . . dead . . .

Like something inhuman.

"Marissa," Ryan whispered, and she began inching along the door, praying the thing couldn't hear her, wouldn't find her, the relentless blare of the horn filling her head, disorienting her in the terrible darkness—

"Marissa," she whispered again, "I didn't mean it . . . I tried to hang on—I—"

From the other side of the garage Marissa's car started up.

Stunned, Ryan realized she'd reached a corner, and she squeezed herself into it, trying to be invisible. She sank to the floor and felt a tiny breath of cold air seeping in under the door.

"Help me," she murmured, and in that split instant she realized that something was near her—beside her in the dark—she could *feel* it—the darkness pulsating with its *presence,* its *danger*—

"Oh, God . . ." She put out her hand and felt heavy, wet fabric . . . damp human skin . . . icy cold . . .

Something slimy coiled around her neck . . .

Shrieking, Ryan's head snapped back and hit the wall, and through the insane darkness, she saw a soft explosion of stars.

Chapter 6

"Ryan? Can you hear me? Come on, open your eyes!"

As Ryan gasped and began to cough, she recognized Charles Eastman's face bending over her. She was lying in the driveway, and as another fit of coughing seized her, Charles began thumping her back and rubbing her face with snow.

"Stop it!" Ryan could hardly speak for choking. "Stop doing that! Let me go!"

"Of course I'm not going to let you go," Charles said patiently. "You'll probably just fall down again."

"What happened? What am I doing out here?"

"Why don't you tell me? I opened the garage door, and you fell out. What'd you do—lock yourself in?"

"The car! Did you turn off the car?"

"What car? My car?"

"No—Marissa's car! The motor—" Ryan struggled to sit up, and Charles obligingly slipped an arm beneath her back. "Someone was in there! Marissa! And she started the motor and I couldn't breathe and she came after me—"

"Whoa, hold on a minute. You're saying someone was in the garage with you?"

"I don't know, I don't know!" Ryan shook her head desperately. "There was a body in the front seat, but it was her! I saw her hair and her ribbons—Oh, God!"

"What's the matter?"

"She came after me—her clothes were wet—she put her ribbon around my neck—"

"There's nothing around your neck."

"But I felt it! Did you look for it? Did you look around?"

"Well, no." Charles looked baffled. "Come on, Ryan, let's get you inside. Lucky for you I started to put my car in here—"

"Lucky for me?" Ryan stared at him. "Lucky for me?" She struggled to push him away, then got clumsily to her feet, falling immediately into his outstretched arms. "Leave me alone!"

"Don't be stupid. If you don't let me help, then I'll have to carry you."

Ryan had no choice. She leaned heavily on Charles as he guided her back to the house, then she collapsed on the couch as he stood back to appraise the situation.

"You stay right here," he ordered. "I'm going to fix you some good strong coffee."

Ryan nodded vacantly, looking past him to one corner of the living room. "You got a tree," she mumbled.

Charles shrugged, brushing it off. "I thought the place needed brightening up. I thought *you* needed brightening up."

Ryan stared at him. "I didn't imagine what happened out there."

"I'll get the coffee," Charles said. "Then we'll talk."

Ryan must have dozed. When she opened her eyes again, Charles was standing over her with two steaming mugs, and she wondered how long he'd been watching her.

"Feel better?" he asked politely.

She gave a halfhearted nod, then ran her fingers cautiously back over her hair. "I hit my head against the door, I think. I was so scared—"

"What happened, did you lock yourself in? When I got there, the door was closed, and when I opened it, you fell right out." Charles gave a grim smile. "Surprised *me*, I'll tell you that."

"Then you must have turned off the horn." Ryan sighed, trying hard to think back, to remember every detail of what had happened.

"What horn?"

"The horn on Marissa's car. It was stuck—that's why I went out there. It was stuck, and when I looked in her car, I saw . . ." She hesitated, swallowing fear. It sounded so preposterous now, she could hardly bring herself to say it. "I saw . . . Marissa."

"Marissa?" Charles's glance was skeptical.

"Yes . . . I mean . . . it looked like her . . . her hair —her ribbons—"

"You saw her face?"

"No . . . the door fell and everything was so black —but she started to get up—I *saw* her! She started to raise her head and—and—"

"Take it easy." Charles regarded her thoughtfully. "She *started* to, but you never actually saw anything."

Ryan shook her head. "No. But she walked toward me. I felt her wet clothes . . . and her skin—"

"She touched you?"

"Well . . . not exactly. I sort of . . . touched her. Accidentally."

"I see."

"But the motor was running by then, and I was all confused—" Ryan was talking fast and Charles was just staring at her, saying nothing. "The horn wouldn't stop, and I hit my head—" She broke off as he got up from his chair and walked slowly over to the tree. "You don't believe me."

He reached out and slowly stroked a branch. "When I got here, I brought the tree inside. Then I went to the garage. There wasn't any horn honking . . . there wasn't any car running. There wasn't anyone—or anything—in there. Except you."

Ryan stared at the cup in her hand. "It was real," she whispered. "I couldn't imagine something that horrible . . . could I?"

"Well . . ." Charles hesitated, his fingers caressing another branch. "It seems to be all tied up with Marissa somehow, doesn't it? Maybe . . . if you talked about her, you'd feel better."

Ryan's voice grew defensive. "Talk about her how?"

"You know." Charles sounded deliberately casual. "Your relationship, for example. Or . . . what you remember most about her. Or . . . what you remember about the time you spent with her before she died."

Ryan's throat closed up and she looked away. "There's nothing to tell. We were . . . you know . . . just sisters."

There was a long silence. Charles sat down on the floor beside the tree and looked at her. "So what's it like, being just sisters? I'm an only child, so it's always seemed special to me. You share a lot? Private jokes? Secrets?"

Ryan nodded. "Yes. Both. Sometimes."

"And she probably confided in you a lot, I bet. Told you stuff she probably wouldn't tell anyone else. . . ."

A flash of memory hit Ryan—that last day in the woods—the secret she'd sworn to keep but never knew—and her eyes brimmed. "Sometimes," she murmured.

"She told me stuff, too," Charles said, and Ryan glanced at him in surprise as he nodded. "Yes, she really did. We were really close friends. She told me lots of things about you."

Ryan glanced away again, feeling suddenly uncomfortable. She didn't want Charles to know anything about her. It made her feel violated somehow.

"She told me about your mom's favoritism." Charles leaned back against the wall and shook his head sadly as Ryan stared at him in disbelief. "I think she really knew you were always being overlooked, that she always got her way, while you just—"

"That's not true!" Ryan said hotly. "Marissa was just the oldest, that's all, she—"

"Ryan," Charles said smoothly, his smile sympathetic, "you don't have to pretend with me, Marissa told me everything. She thought you were really special, you know."

Ryan felt trapped. She shifted on the couch and spilled coffee on her sweater. She dabbed at it with her sleeve.

"Your turn," Charles said from his corner.

"My turn what?" Ryan said jumpily.

"I've told you things Marissa told *me*—now why don't you tell me something she told *you*? We'll trade."

"I don't want to trade." Ryan set her mug down on the floor. "I want to go upstairs."

"It might help, you know," Charles said softly. When Ryan didn't answer, he tried again. "Whatever happened out there tonight—maybe if you talked about her, all the ghosts would go away."

"I don't want to." Ryan shook her head fiercely. "I don't need to."

She was almost to the door when his voice stopped her.

"But *I* need to."

Surprised, Ryan faced him. He was gazing down into his cup, and his lips were pressed in a troubled frown.

"I need to, Ryan," he said again, avoiding her eyes. "I need to know what her last day was like . . . her last hours. What she did . . . what she talked about . . ." His eyes raised at last as his voice lowered. "If she was happy."

Again the memory came back—Marissa's voice, her odd behavior. *"I think I'm in trouble . . . serious trouble—"*

"But it doesn't matter now," Ryan mumbled. "It doesn't matter because she's gone, and I'll never know what she was talking about—"

"What?"

She frowned, not realizing she'd spoken aloud or that Charles had heard. "Nothing."

"You said she was talking about something . . ." Charles spoke carefully. "Don't shut me out, Ryan. I care about her, too."

"I can't." Ryan turned again and started for the hall. "I can't talk about her. Maybe someday. But not now."

She jumped as Charles grabbed her elbow. She hadn't even heard him get up or cross the room.

"When you *do* feel like it," he said, "talk to me, Ryan."

She stared into his face, saw his half smile, winced as his fingers tightened on her arm.

"I'm here for you," Charles whispered. "It would mean so *much* to me."

Chapter 7

So," Mrs. McCauley said. "Do you want to tell me what happened?"

Ryan sat up, blinking against the light, and saw her mother standing rigidly beside the bed. A quick glance at the clock told her she'd only been napping an hour, but her head felt like it had been in a coma for weeks.

"I fell in the garage," she mumbled.

"And hit your head. Charles told me." Mrs. McCauley sighed.

Then why bother to ask? "I'm okay now," Ryan added.

"I'd hardly call hallucinating okay." Mrs. McCauley bowed her head, her fingers plucking at the hem of her skirt. "Actually, I'm glad we're talking. There's something I think you should know about."

"What?"

"I had a talk with Mrs. Corbett this afternoon—"

"The school counselor? Why?"

"Don't get upset, Ryan, everything is *all right*. She called and asked if I had a minute, so I went by." Mrs.

McCauley's fingers twisted more tightly, but Ryan couldn't see her expression. "She's . . . disturbed about you."

She's disturbed . . . that's really funny . . . I'm losing my mind, and she's disturbed . . . "What'd she say?" Ryan was apprehensive.

"It's about school," Mrs. McCauley said slowly. "Your grades . . . how you're so distracted . . . depressed . . ." Her voice trailed away. "I told her it hasn't been easy for any of us. That you have all this . . . this"—she made a frustrated gesture —*"guilt.* And of course she understands, but she thinks maybe it would help—"

"Guilt?" Ryan echoed as her mother glanced at her. "And what do you say, Mom, about this *guilt* of mine?"

"Mrs. Corbett says it's normal, your having these lapses in class, perfectly normal, after what happened to Marissa—"

"I didn't let her drown," Ryan whispered, and she hated her mother in that split second for tearing her eyes away, for not looking at her, for letting seconds go by before she answered.

"Of course you didn't, Ryan, for God's sake, nobody thinks—"

Mrs. McCauley jumped as there was a knock on the door and Steve peered in.

"Phoebe's here. She says you're supposed to go caroling."

"I don't want to go." Ryan threw back the covers and moved past both of them into the hall.

"You're going!" Phoebe's voice carried up from downstairs. "I'm not going if you don't go!"

"Then stay home!" Ryan yelled down.

"You can't do this to me! I told you we're all going to Michael Kilmer's afterward." Phoebe bounded up the stairs and confronted Ryan with her most desperate look. "You've *got* to go! My whole *future* depends on it!"

"Oh, go on, Ryan." Steve grinned. "I'm driving your mom over to Morrisville to see her friends, anyway. And you wouldn't want Phoebe's tragic future on your conscience. . . ." His voice trailed off as his grin faded. Carefully he reached out and touched Ryan's head, giving a long, low whistle. "Wow . . . is this where you hit yourself?"

"Yes," Ryan grumbled. "When I fell."

"Well, you must have fallen awful hard." Steve looked concerned. "If I didn't know better, I'd say someone hit—"

"Well, hello!" interrupted a cheery voice. "Am I missing something exciting?"

Grouped at the head of the stairs, they all turned as Ryan's bedroom door opened and Charles peered out in surprise. Ryan saw the gleam in Phoebe's eyes and gave an inward groan.

"Maybe." Phoebe dimpled. "You must be Charles."

"Ah, so you've heard of me." He cast Ryan an amused look. "And you're undoubtedly the one and only Phoebe I've heard so much about."

Great, Mom, what else have you told him about our lives? Ryan closed her eyes. *No, Phoebe, don't—*

"We're going caroling. Want to come?"

"He'd be bored," Ryan said.

"I don't think he would." Mrs. McCauley smiled. "I think it's a fine idea. Go ahead, Charles, it'll be fun."

"Michael's not expecting another guest," Ryan broke in.

"Oh, he won't care!" Phoebe's dimples deepened as Charles reached out to shake her hand. "Lots of kids are coming. Dad even loaned me the van. Please come. You can be Ryan's date!"

"No," Ryan said.

"Well . . . I was going to ask Ryan to show me around town tonight, but . . . sure. I'd love to." Charles smiled, casting Ryan a sly glance. "Come on, Ryan, we're practically old friends. Don't be shy."

"This isn't a date thing," Ryan said quickly and saw Steve throw her a sympathetic look. "It's just a bunch of kids getting together. No dates."

"Don't wait up for Ryan, Mrs. McCauley! She can spend the night at my house!" Phoebe's hand was still locked in Charles's, and she began to pull him downstairs. "Oh, I'm so glad you said yes!"

"Me, too," Charles said smoothly. "I haven't been caroling since I was a kid. I probably won't even remember the songs."

"We'll teach you." Phoebe nodded eagerly. "Won't we, Ryan?"

"You can," Ryan tossed back. "You're so good at stuff like that."

"Okay. I don't mind a bit!"

As the threesome bundled up and trooped outside,

Ryan cast a miserable look back at the porch. Mom looked happy, but Steve had an uneasy expression that matched the way Ryan felt.

"I just love this time of year, don't you?" Phoebe chattered as she headed the van through town. "All the Christmas decorations—everything's so beautiful. Especially in the snow."

Ryan huddled in the back, where she didn't have to talk to Charles. It startled her when he reached back and patted her shoulder, then turned around to smile.

"I love the snow, too. So clean and pure."

"I don't even mind driving in it. Not like ice," Phoebe babbled. "I hate driving on ice."

"Ice," Charles murmured. "It's so dangerous, ice. So scary."

"Let's not talk about ice," Phoebe said quickly. "Let's talk about you."

"There's nothing to tell, really. I lead an extremely boring life."

"You don't look boring," Phoebe's glance was coy. "What do you like to do?"

"The unexpected." Charles's smile broadened. "I'm a great believer in surprises."

"Ooh, I like that!" Phoebe giggled. "Most guys are so predictable."

"Are they?" Charles shrugged. "I like to think I'm not like other guys."

"Oh, look!" Phoebe honked the horn and waved. "There's everybody over there!" In her excitement the van went too quickly around a corner, and Phoebe slid into Charles.

"Hey, it's okay." He grinned. "It's a nice change having a girl throw herself at me." As Phoebe laughed, Charles glanced back at Ryan, but she looked away.

The evening should have been fun, but to Ryan it was only an endless blur. As she listlessly trailed the merry group of carolers up and down neighborhood streets, she felt conspicuously separate from everyone else. Phoebe and Michael were snuggled up together, singing offkey harmony, and every time Ryan looked up, Charles was watching her with a concerned smile. She tried to beg off from the party, but Phoebe wouldn't hear of it, and once they'd reached Michael's house miles out in the country, she resigned herself to being trapped. With the party in full swing around her, Ryan finally managed to find an empty room and settled herself down to wait.

"So there you are," a voice greeted her from the doorway, and her heart sank as Charles sat beside her. "You're missing out on all the fun."

"I want to miss the fun." Ryan leaned back and shut her eyes. "I don't feel much like fun right now."

When he didn't answer, she opened her eyes and looked at him. He was smiling and holding out a cup.

"No, thank you," she said.

"Oh, go on, drink it. It's only hot cider."

"I don't want it."

Charles sighed and set the cup down on the table in front of her. "I'll leave it here in case you change your mind."

He had started back toward the door, but now he

stopped and faced her, and the hurt on his face caught her off-guard.

"You know," Charles said slowly, "if I hadn't shown up when I did at the house earlier, you might have frozen to death. At the very least, you could have ended up with pneumonia." A muscle moved in his jaw, and his voice lowered. "I don't understand why you're acting this way. I don't think I deserve it."

As Ryan stared, Charles opened his mouth as if to say more, then seemed to change his mind. He let himself out, closing the door behind him.

Taken aback, Ryan sat there, her mind in a whirl. She could still see the expression on his face, hear the confusion in his voice. *I've been acting so mean to him.* She remembered him offering to change rooms with her . . . talking so sweetly about Marissa . . . bringing the Christmas tree . . . *"I thought you needed brightening up. . . ."*

"Oh, Ryan, you're such a bitch sometimes," she groaned. So what if Charles seemed a little self-centered—maybe he was really insecure and that was his way of covering up. *Maybe he really is hurting about Marissa—just as much as me. . . .*

Ryan picked up the cider and sipped it. No matter how different Charles seemed, that didn't give her the right to be rude. *Especially when he really might have saved my life tonight.* Not wanting to think any more about her close call, Ryan downed the rest of her drink and went out to join the others.

The party was getting wilder by the minute. Charles

didn't seem to be anywhere around, and Ryan caught up with Phoebe in the kitchen.

"Phoebe, have you seen Charles?"

"He was here a minute ago, and I wondered why you weren't with him. Okay, what happened?"

"Nothing. I told you before, he's not my date."

"Well, you'd better get smart and latch on to him. He's *cute!* And he has nice manners, unlike most of the heathens around here."

"Are you speaking of Michael, too?" Ryan teased.

"If *you're* not interested in Charles, *I* could be," Phoebe retorted. "All that beautiful blond hair—and that smile—"

"Look, Phoebe, if you see Charles, just tell him I'm looking for him, okay?"

Phoebe pretended to be deep in thought. "Hmmm . . . this sounds almost promising—"

"Just do it." Ryan chuckled. She started through the doorway when the room suddenly tilted around her.

Shocked, Ryan grabbed at the doorframe, her stomach lurching, her heart pounding in a frantic race. Above her the ceiling turned upside down, and around her the furniture went topsy-turvy. Her legs turned to rubber, and she sat down hard on the floor.

"Phoebe"—she tried to shout, but her mouth was all cottony—"Phoebe—oh!"

If she hadn't felt so dizzy, she would have laughed at herself hugging the wall, even though she'd already fallen onto the floor. She *wanted* to laugh, it was so ridiculous, and as she tried to boost herself up, she heard Phoebe's voice close to her ear.

"Oh, Charles, what's *wrong* with her? Is she okay?"

"She's fine. Come on, now, Ryan, I've got you, up you go—"

"Ryan, what's wrong?" And there was Phoebe's face, all distorted like a funny mask, and Charles's face blurry beside it. "Oh, don't let anyone see her like this, she'd be so embarrassed!"

"Phoebe." Ryan reached for her friend's arm, but her own hand fell uselessly away. "I really need to go home, okay?"

"What did you do, Ryan? Did you drink something? Did you eat something bad? Are you sick?"

"No, I always look like this!" Ryan heard herself laughing and saw Phoebe and Charles exchange looks. "Oh—oh—the room's going again. I'm going with it—"

"Catch her!" Phoebe yelled at Charles. "Oh, God, Ryan, I've got to get you home. Did you take something? Medicine? What's *wrong* with her, Charles?"

Ryan tugged on her sleeve. "You'll have to drive me home."

Phoebe nodded, helping Charles hold Ryan up. "Okay, wait just a second while I tell Michael—"

"Come on, Phoebe, there's no reason for you to leave," Charles broke in. "I'm ready to call it a night anyway. I can borrow your car and bring it back."

"No, just keep it. Take Ryan home, and I'll get a ride and pick up the van tomorrow." Phoebe glanced worriedly at Ryan's glazed expression. "Do you think she'll be okay?"

Charles accepted the keys Phoebe handed him. "She didn't feel too good earlier. This is probably just a delayed reaction. Don't worry—she probably just needs some sleep."

Ryan felt chilled to the bone and could hardly feel herself walking to the van. She leaned against Charles as Phoebe gave him directions and hurriedly piled blankets on the floor.

"You lie down and bundle up back here, Ryan," Phoebe insisted. "Then you can sleep on the way."

"Good thinking," Charles said admiringly. "Everyone should have such a good friend."

"That's what I keep telling her." Phoebe chuckled and waved as they took off.

Ryan felt like a sack of lead. She was conscious of the hard floor beneath her and the mountain of blankets on top of her, but her mind was too fuzzy to comprehend more. The only sounds were the motor's hum, the whine of the heater, and the tick of the wipers brushing snow. As she gave in to the rocking motion of the van, her eyes grew unbearably heavy. When she came to, it was because of something sensed rather than known, and as she struggled to sit up, she saw Charles leaning forward, squinting through the windshield.

"What's the matter?" Ryan mumbled. "Where are we?"

Charles's look was concerned but calm. "To tell you the truth, I'm not sure. I think we might be lost."

"What? We can't be."

Ryan strained to see through the fogged-up windows. It was snowing again—even harder than before—and nothing in the landscape looked even remotely familiar.

"What'd you do?" She turned accusing eyes on him, and he gave a sheepish shrug.

"I don't know. I must've taken a wrong turn somewhere. Stop looking at me like that—you act like I did it on purpose."

"There weren't any turns to take until we hit town. Stop the car." Her heart was racing now, danger signals coursing through her body.

"But—"

"Stop the car! I mean it, Charles, stop it right—"

Her sentence was jolted from her as Charles yanked the wheel and the van slid sideways. Ryan hit the floor and felt the van fishtail, straighten out, then skid. There was a heavy thud as they stopped, and then she heard Charles cursing as he threw off his seat belt and shoved open the door.

"Stay here," he ordered, even as Ryan struggled to follow.

"I will not," she said groggily. "You're crazy, you know that? People like you shouldn't be allowed out on the road."

"A dog ran right in front of me. What'd you expect me to do—kill it?"

"Did you hit it?" Ryan asked anxiously. She was so dizzy, she could hardly hold her head up. *I feel like I've been drugged.* . . . "Where are you going?"

"To check the van." Charles disappeared for several minutes, then his face reappeared in the window, his expression tense. "This is great. I think we have a flat. *And* a missing hubcap."

"What about the dog?"

"What do I care about a damn dog? I've got to get us out of here."

"Well, what are you going to do?"

"I'm going to try and find that hubcap, and then I'm going to try and fix the tire, if the tools are here to do it with."

"Oh, they're probably not." Ryan groaned, and fell back onto the blankets. "Jinx is always using them, and Mr. Evans is always yelling at him to put them back, and he's always forgetting."

"Well, just stay put." She could hear him walking away, and she pulled herself up to the front and tried to yell at him.

"Why don't you see if you can find that dog?"

"Ryan, I mean it—stay inside and keep the window up. And get under those blankets. It's freezing out here."

Ryan listened for several minutes more. She could hear him muttering, and as she craned her neck through the window, she saw him walking farther and farther from the car, his head lowered, searching the ground. With all her strength she managed to inch open the door and get out. *I wonder if he really did hit that dog. The poor thing could be lying out here in the cold. . . .*

The temperature had dropped a lot in the past few

hours. Ryan gasped as the first icy blast hit her and she started walking unsteadily. *If we skidded from over there, then the dog must be around here. . . .*

The snow was heavy and wet, already changing the landscape with deceptive drifts. Ryan blinked snow from her lashes and shielded her face with one hand, scanning the white fields for some sign of movement. *Maybe it was just a shadow Charles saw. . . . Maybe there really wasn't a dog at all, and he just thought he hit something. . . .* She couldn't bear to think of any creature lying out here, hurt and frightened and alone in the dark. She cupped her hands and whistled softly.

"Here, dog! Come on—good dog!"

Straining her ears, Ryan heard deep, heavy silence. . . .

And then something that made her heart stop.

"Oh, no," Ryan whispered, "oh, no, oh, no—" and she began to run, painfully slow motion in the suffocating snow, gasping, trying to scream "Charles! Charles!" over and over again, her cries swallowed in a swirling white fog. . . .

It wasn't the dog she heard . . . that whining sound growing fainter and fainter in the distance . . .

It was the van as it drove away into the snowy night.

Chapter 8

My God, he's left me here. . . .

In slow realization Ryan reached out and anchored herself against a sturdy tree.

I don't believe this . . . he's left me here to freeze to death.

She had no idea where she was. As her frightened eyes tried to see past the thickening snow, she searched desperately for a light . . . a sign of chimney smoke against the pale sky . . . some small sign of hope. *The tire tracks . . . I'll just follow the tracks—*

Her legs took over then, mechanically, steering her along. *Someone will miss me and worry about me and come looking for me and—*She suddenly remembered that no one would even notice her absence till morning—Phoebe thought she'd gone home for the night, and Mom thought she'd be at Phoebe's and *what will Charles be doing in the meantime, what story will he be making up about how he managed to lose me out in the middle of nowhere . . . ?*

Ryan stopped, staring helplessly at the white terrain stretching ahead of her, the van's tire tracks covered in fresh snow as if they had never existed. "Damn you, Charles Eastman!" she sobbed. *"Damn you!"*

For a split second she was so consumed by panic that she had to forcibly restrain herself from just dashing off into the whirling white oblivion. *Try to think, Ryan, try to think . . . think and keep walking . . . don't stop moving . . .* She remembered reading somewhere that snow could actually keep you warm, and as she kept doggedly on, she tried to concentrate on the millions of tiny flakes, imagining them as little white coals, surrounding her with heat. She thought of Phoebe's kitchen . . . the Evanses' Christmas tree . . . her own room safe at home—*No, Charles is there*— and Mr. Partini's toy shop—*Someone was watching at the window, someone tried to scare me with the dollhouse*—and suddenly she was thinking of Marissa and that last day—

"Ryan," a voice called softly, "Ryaaaan . . . come to me . . ."

Ryan stopped so suddenly that she nearly fell. A shiver went up her spine, far more chilling than the cold.

"Hello?" she called shakily. "Is someone there?"

The wind gusted through the bare trees, sending a flurry into her eyes. Ryan's hand went slowly to her face, and she tried to blink the snow away.

"Ryaaan . . ." And there it was again, that strange, lifeless voice, calling . . .

Ryan's lips moved but made no sound. As she stared off into the swirling darkness, a white, filmy shape began to gather itself from the snow. . . .

It was floating toward her.

She saw the long, flowing hair . . . the fluttering clothes . . . the arms lifting . . . reaching out . . .

"Ryaaan," the voice wept, "why did you let me drown?"

And even from this distance Ryan could see the flickering light it gave out, the dying light that surrounded it—

"I can't come home for Christmas, Ryan . . . I'm dead. . . ."

"No!" Ryan shrieked. *"Marissa! No!"*

She ran in a directionless frenzy until her body refused to run anymore. Without warning she slid headfirst down an embankment into shallow, icy water and lay there, stunned, as the snow covered her.

She didn't hear the heavy boots stirring the drifts around her, stopping beside her face.

She didn't even try to look up.

She only knew she was warm now.

Chapter 9

The first things Ryan saw were orange and red shadows flickering in quiet patterns up a wall. Then she heard a soft crackle of firewood . . . a sputter of flame . . . and the hiss of falling ashes. She felt layers of thick blankets upon her and soft pillows beneath her head, and she realized she was lying in a bed she didn't recognize, in a room she didn't know. She also realized her clothes were gone.

"So you're awake."

A soft voice startled her from the shadows, and she clutched the blankets tightly to her chin.

"You need to rest," the voice said again. "You should sleep as much as you can."

It was someone she knew but couldn't quite place. She stared apprehensively toward the sound and at last was able to pick out a figure kneeling in front of a fireplace. Shadowy hands snapped twigs and fed them into the flames, and a face turned into the light.

"Don't be afraid," Winchester said. "I won't hurt you."

Ryan felt numb. All she could do was stare.

"Do you remember anything?" he asked softly. "I found you outside about half a mile from here. You were soaking wet and practically frozen. Pretty cut up, too."

"My . . . clothes," she mumbled.

"They'll be dry by morning." He nodded toward the fireplace, where her things were draped neatly over a screen. "Are you warm enough?"

Ryan continued to stare at him in disbelief, and he went on.

"My dog came home hurt—looked like he might have been hit by a car. We don't get much traffic back here—mostly people who end up lost and can't find their way to the main road. Anyway, I went out to see if anyone might be in trouble."

"A . . . car?" Ryan finally said. "Your dog?"

"Oh, he's okay," Winchester assured her. "Just a few scratches. Better than I can say for you." As if to reassure her, he gestured to a corner near the fire. Ryan hadn't noticed the dog before, but now the big shepherd thumped his tail amicably and regarded her with sleepy eyes.

"Then . . . he really did hit a dog," she whispered.

"What?" Winchester moved closer. "What is it?"

Ryan lowered her eyes, shaking her head slowly. "I hurt all over. I don't understand. . . . How did you—"

"Then you *do* remember me." His smile was shy and slow, like his voice. He stopped several feet from the bed, as if afraid of frightening her.

"Of course I remember you." Ryan chanced a quick look at him. "But I still don't—"

"I live here," he said quietly. *"We* live here. My dad, my brothers and sisters—and—" He nodded to the dog.

"Your dad has the garage in town," Ryan said stupidly.

"That's right."

"And you . . . live here?"

"We're so far out from town—on nights like this, Dad usually just sleeps at the station."

"So . . . he's not here?"

Winchester shook his head, firelight gleaming on his hair, black as ravens' wings. "I have to watch the kids tonight," he said after a moment. "They're upstairs asleep."

"And your mom . . . she's not home, either?"

He glanced away. "She died two years ago."

"Oh . . . I'm sorry."

Ryan scanned the dimly lit room and noticed several closed doors. "How old are the kids?"

"All of them?" He squinted, doing a tabulation in his head. "Three to ten. They don't mind staying alone when I have to help Dad, but a couple of them came down sick tonight."

Again Ryan took a quick inventory of the room. It looked like a big log cabin, with wood walls and Indian rugs and old comfortable chairs around the hearth. She could hear the wind whining outside, and a stray gust whooshed down the chimney, scattering sparks. Winchester bent over and crushed them calmly beneath the toe of his boot.

"I'm sorry about your brothers and sisters," Ryan said.

He shrugged philosophically. "Probably the flu. I just hope you don't catch it."

"I . . . I guess you're wondering what I was doing out here." Ryan watched as Winchester came closer and put one hand gently to her forehead. "I know this is going to sound really crazy."

His hand slid away. He straightened the covers around her shoulders. "All that matters is that you're okay."

Ryan regarded him for a long time, but he kept his eyes on the blankets. "I'd like to go home," she said and was surprised when he shook his head.

"I wish I could take you, but I'm stranded here without a car. And I can't call anyone for you because the line's out." He looked softly troubled. "Your mom's going to have a sleepless night worrying about you."

"She doesn't even know . . ." Ryan began, and suddenly tears filled her eyes, spilling down her cheeks. She felt the bed move slightly as Winchester sat down on the edge.

"Don't cry," he said gently. "I promise you'll be safe here. And I'll take you home in the morning as soon as my dad gets back with the truck."

"It's not that," Ryan choked. "It doesn't matter about that . . . only . . ."

"Only what?"

"I saw my sister out there tonight. I saw Marissa."

For a long moment there was silence.

"Your sister," Winchester said at last, and he stared hard into the flames.

"I know it sounds crazy. But she was there in the woods—before you found me—" She broke off as his eyes fell full upon her face.

"Come sit by the fire," he said quietly. He wiped her tears with one corner of the blanket. "Pull these tight around you—I'll carry you."

Before she could protest, Ryan felt herself being lifted into his arms, being carried across the floor as if she were weightless. Winchester lowered her gently onto the rug beside the hearth and put pillows at her back so she could rest but still see the fire.

"Are you comfortable?" He tucked the covers around her once more, and when she nodded, he stretched out on his side, crossing his long legs. "Now. Tell me what happened."

"I saw Marissa tonight. In the woods." Ryan hesitated. "The guy I was riding with drove off and left me after he hit your dog."

Winchester's eyes were calm, intent on the fire. He roused himself slightly but didn't look at her.

"Then you weren't alone?"

"No. We'd been to a party, and I got sick, and he was supposed to take me home. He just left me! And then Marissa came. . . ."

There was an uneasy silence. Finally Winchester shook his head.

"There's no way Marissa could have survived in

that river under the ice. The current's too strong . . . the water's too cold." He leaned forward so slowly that she didn't actually see him move at all, just felt the sudden warmth of his body against hers. "You'll never see her again, Ryan. She's gone."

Ryan ducked her head but immediately felt his fingers beneath her chin, forcing her to look up at him. His eyes were compassionate, and they seemed to peer into her soul.

"I thought I saw her in my garage today." Ryan forced a laugh. "Can you imagine? It's like I can't get away from her. Like she won't stay out of my mind."

"Then maybe you should talk about her," Winchester said slowly. "Maybe there's something bothering you that you need to let go of."

Ryan swallowed tears. "I just wish that last day had been different, you know? I was mad at her." She closed her eyes, trying to shut out the memories. "She was so upset—"

"About what?"

"I don't know! She never told me! I thought she was joking, so I walked away and left her, and she—she started screaming. . . ." Ryan twisted her face from his grasp. "Oh, what does it matter anyway? I wish I could forget about it—but I *can't!*"

Winchester pulled away . . . stared into the fire. "So . . . you really believe now that something was bothering her?"

"Maybe if I'd taken her seriously, she would have told me. I swore I'd keep it a secret, but I never knew what it was." Ryan leaned back and closed her eyes. "I don't even know why I'm telling you this."

A log fell in the fireplace with a muffled thud. Golden light danced over Winchester's hair.

Ryan sighed. "I'm so tired."

She felt Winchester's arms go around her once more, lifting her, carrying her across the room, placing her carefully back into bed. She held the covers close as he stood back.

"Thank you," she murmured, "for finding me."

"Sleep now."

She watched him, wanting to say more, not knowing how. She glanced over at her clothes on the fireguard and felt a blush spread over her cheeks.

Winchester followed the direction of her stare, and a faint smile played at the corners of his mouth.

"I kept my eyes closed," he said quietly. "Good night."

Chapter 10

Ryan awoke to pale gray light and the smell of bacon and coffee. Rubbing her eyes, she started to sit up, then dived back under the covers as the door opened and Winchester appeared with his arms full of firewood, stamping snow off his boots. He nodded and kicked the door shut.

"I thought you might be hungry."

"Is your father home?"

"He's out in the shed."

"I guess he must be thinking who-knows-what—"

"He thinks I rescued you from the snowstorm." Winchester dropped the logs into the woodbox by the hearth. "Which is exactly what happened, isn't it?"

Ryan stared at him as he knelt on the rug and busied himself stirring the fire. He shrugged out of his denim jacket and shook his windblown hair from his eyes.

"I'd really like to go home now," she said.

"Sure. As soon as you eat something."

"Could you hand me my clothes?"

He tossed her jeans and sweater onto the bed, hardly looking at her. Without a word he got up and went outside again, leaving Ryan in a brief moment of privacy.

Pain swept through her body the moment her feet touched the floor. She dressed as quickly as she could, then limped over and knelt in front of the fireplace. She held her hands to the coals, savoring their delicious warmth, and was startled when Winchester leaned in beside her to pitch in another log.

"Oh! I didn't hear you come in!"

"You're still cold." He sounded concerned and in a moment had coaxed the flames to a crackling inferno. "Stay right here. I'll bring your food."

Ryan made a face as she examined the scrapes on her hands and arms, as she gingerly touched the scratches on her cheeks. "I really am a mess, aren't I?" she grumbled.

Winchester gave a half smile. "Not to me, you're not." As he began buttering toast, one of the doors opened, and a child's tousled head poked through.

"Hi," the little girl said, her huge eyes on Ryan.

"Hi, yourself." Ryan smiled back.

"I'm Katy," the child said, looking from Ryan to Winchester, then back again.

"Go back to bed," Winchester said softly.

Katy looked at him as if trying to decide how much leeway she had with his instructions. She stared at Ryan. "Did you sleep here last night?"

"Yes." Ryan nodded.

"Where?"

"There." Ryan pointed, and the child giggled.

"With Winchester?"

"No!" Ryan's face reddened, and Winchester's voice sounded again.

"Bed, Katy. Now." This time there was no mistaking the orders. Katy waved and promptly disappeared.

Ryan sighed as Winchester handed her a plate. "I guess . . . there's some explaining to do."

Winchester seemed amused. "That *is* my bed."

"Your bed!"

"Well, we're pretty cramped for space here." He sat on the floor and balanced a cup of coffee on one knee. "Her comment was perfectly innocent."

Smiling, Ryan tackled her food. There were muffled thumps from the ceiling, and Winchester went to the door where Katy had been, his voice firm but calm.

"I better not have to come up there! Stay in bed!"

Ryan chuckled. "How are they this morning?"

"Bored." Winchester closed the door again and shook his head. "When you're finished, we can go."

The snow had stopped, but the sky threatened more. As Ryan followed Winchester out to the shed, she sank up to her knees several times in deep drifts and had to be rescued. The last time Winchester pulled her out, she ended up against his chest with his arms around her to keep her from falling. She didn't pull back right away, and he didn't let her go until a cheery voice boomed out from the shed.

"Well! Hello, there, young lady! I hear you need yourself a lift home!"

Flustered, Ryan disentangled herself from Winchester's arms and saw Mr. Stone grinning at them.

"I'm really sorry about this," she began, but he pumped both her hands easily in one big paw.

"No bother at all! Just as soon as I finish up here, we'll be ready to hit the road. I brought Mrs. Larsen to look after the kids"—he winked—"but don't worry—I sent her in the back way, and she'll never know you've been here!"

"As if Katy will keep her mouth shut," Winchester said in mock seriousness, and Ryan looked away, flustered.

Ten minutes later, with the three of them squeezed tightly into the tow truck, Ryan tried to ignore Winchester's arm resting along the top of the seat over her shoulders.

"I hope you fed this pretty little thing some breakfast." Mr. Stone chuckled, glancing at his son.

Winchester nodded and stared out the window.

"I went back down to the field and had me a look around," Mr. Stone went on, smiling broadly out the windshield. "Damn, it's a beautiful morning! Didn't see a thing out there—no tire tracks, nothing busted. 'Course, wouldn't expect to find anything after a snow like this." He took a deep breath of crisp morning air. "Still, doesn't hurt to check it out."

Ryan glanced sharply at Winchester.

"What's he talking about?"

"And if you *had* a car, I sure couldn't find it." Mr. Stone glanced over, his smile widening, and covered one of her hands with his huge one. "You know, sometimes when we've had a little too much to handle, we can dream all kinds of things—"

"What?" Ryan looked from Winchester to his father and back again. "Are you saying I was drinking?"

"Shoot, you kids just don't realize what it can do—"

"But—but—I don't even *drink* and—"

"Just drop it, Dad, okay?" Winchester sighed. He'd never taken his eyes from the window, and now Ryan grabbed his arm.

"Do you think I made it all up? Do you think—"

"We're just trying to find out what really happened to you. That's all, little lady, that's all it is." Mr. Stone smiled again.

"But I told you! The guy I was with just drove away and left me—"

"And you saw Marissa. I remember. She came out of the woods and you ran." Winchester finally looked at her, and Ryan felt herself redden.

"That's what happened. Yes."

"We just want to make sure you didn't have a car out here somewhere," Mr. Stone said, trying to soothe her. "That you didn't have yourself a wreck and wandered away and forgot it."

Ryan didn't speak the rest of the way home. As Winchester climbed out to help her down, Ryan pulled out of his grasp.

"Thanks for the ride," she said stiffly. "Thanks for everything."

She tried to slam the door, but he was blocking it.

"Ryan—wait—"

"You don't believe a single thing I told you! You think I was drunk and lost my car!"

"That's not true—I don't think that—"

"I can't believe I trusted you! And let me tell you something else—it wasn't a joke, either, me being left out there—he did it on purpose!"

Ryan ran for the house, but she could tell before she even got inside that no one was home. Her mind spun in a hundred directions, and she could feel her fears going out of control. *What should I do? Call the police? Run away? What's Charles going to do when he sees me? Why won't anyone believe me—*

Something stirred on the floor above.

Ryan froze at the foot of the stairs, her heart racing.

"Mom?" she whispered. "Is that you?"

There was no one in her mother's bedroom. As Ryan peered in fearfully, she saw the curtains billowing against the wall, and she felt weak with relief.

She walked slowly to Marissa's room and took a deep, steadying breath.

The door swung open easily, yet Ryan stood where she was.

The room was cold and full of shadows. Ryan rubbed the chill from her arms and suddenly noticed something on the bed.

A package.

As she frowned and picked it up, she saw that it was wrapped in Christmas paper and that the tag had her name on it. *It must be one of the things Charles brought. Mom must have put it in here for me to open in private. . . .*

Sitting down on the bed, Ryan began unwrapping the small, square box. She lay the paper aside and tried to smooth out the wrinkles. Then she held her breath and lifted the lid.

And at first she wasn't sure what she was seeing—the little gold chain lying on shiny black satin—but as she kept staring at it, she realized what it was, that she had seen it so many times before, and that she *shouldn't* be seeing it now—

"Marissa's necklace," Ryan whispered. "No—it's not possible—"

The box shook violently in her hands, and her thoughts spun back to that last fatal day, and *Marissa with her necklace on . . . the necklace she always wore —and my God, it was around her neck that day. . . . How can it be here now—*

With a horrified cry, Ryan dropped the box and ran. And as she flung open the front door and saw Charles standing there, she felt his arms clamp around her like a steel trap.

Chapter 11

Ryan!" Charles gasped. "My God—you're alive!"

As Ryan stared into his shocked face, she gave him a shove and dashed past him out across the yard.

"Ryan! Come back here!"

She could hear him shouting, and she tried to run faster, but the deep snow slowed her down. She heard his breathing, and she began to scream.

"No! Get away from me!"

Something grabbed her ankles, and as she pitched forward, his body pinned her to the ground.

"Stop it, Ryan!" Charles shouted. "I don't blame you for being upset—but listen to me, will you?"

"I will *not!*" She was beside herself with panic. "You tried to *kill* me! I'm calling the *police!*"

He slammed her shoulders down. "Fine! Call them! They'll be glad to know you finally showed up! Where have you *been?*"

"Stop it! You're just disappointed I'm not a corpse by now!"

She struggled to free herself, but he was too strong. As his face bent closer, his eyes bored into hers with a chilling intensity.

"I've been up . . . all . . . night . . . long," he said slowly, each word hissing between clenched teeth. "I have been scared out of my *mind!* I finally got back here last night, and you weren't in the van! I didn't even know how to get back to where I'd lost you!"

"You're a liar," Ryan said. "I don't believe you."

"Just shut up and listen." Charles was really angry, and she winced from his pressure on her arms. "I don't know when—or from where—you decided to hitchhike home. All I know is that I thought you were buried under all those blankets, only you weren't in the van when I got back last night! I couldn't remember where we'd gone off the road—I drove around for hours—I got stuck in the snow—I slid into things— not to mention all the times I got lost all over again!"

His eyes glittered fiercely, and Ryan stared back in confusion.

"I finally came home and waited for the storm to let up. Then I had to wait for the roads to be cleared. And *then* I finally *did* find the road again, but you weren't *anywhere!* So I got out and *walked* . . . and *called* . . . but you were *gone!* Dammit, Ryan, I thought you were dead!"

Ryan gazed at him helplessly. "And . . . you really called the police?"

"What kind of person do you think I am, anyway?" he shot back. "No . . . never mind. Don't answer that." He released her and straightened up. "You've been wanting to build a case against me ever since I got here. Come on, Ryan, I want to know what your problem is. All I wanted to do was bring Marissa's presents, and it's turned into a visit to hell! I don't blame you for being mad about last night—but how do you think *I* felt! I've been in a *panic,* wondering what to do, wondering what I could tell your mother and Steve—"

"Where are they?" Ryan mumbled. "Where's Mom?"

"She had to stay over at her friend's house last night because of the snow."

"How do you know that?"

"There was a message on the machine. She tried to call Steve at his house to tell him the roads were closed, and not to come and get her, but she couldn't get him there, so she left a message for him on the machine here."

"So you listened in on our phone calls?"

"I thought it might be you! Or the police! God, I was—" He broke off abruptly, running one hand through his hair. Ryan heard him make a disgusted sound in his throat as he got up and yanked her roughly to her feet. "Forget it, Ryan, it's no use talking to you, since you already have some twisted idea about me in your head. Whatever that idea is." Charles turned and started away, and Ryan hurried after him.

"Wait! Where are you going?"

"To call the police. To let them know you're home safe, however the hell that happened—"

"Charles!" Ryan was hurrying to keep up with his long strides, but he wouldn't slow down. "Charles, wait! I'm sorry!"

He did slow down then. As she covered the last few feet to his side, he looked back at her, his eyes so . . . so *hurt*, Ryan thought with a shock—*I've hurt his feelings, and all this time—*

"I'm sorry," she said again. She reached slowly for his hand, and he stared down as her fingers closed around his. "It's just that . . ." Tears welled in her throat, and she took a long moment to bring her voice under control. "It's just that I've been so scared and . . . and . . . so—" She glanced toward the house and tried to suppress a shudder. "I'm really scared, Charles. I don't know what to think—"

His expression hovered between bewilderment and concern. She could tell he didn't want to give in to her apology, but then she felt him squeezing her fingers.

"Ryan . . . what's wrong? You look so—"

"It's Marissa."

"Marissa?"

"That package you brought—it doesn't make sense! Her necklace was in it, but it couldn't have been, don't you see? She was *wearing* that necklace the day she died—she *never* took it off—"

"Whoa, whoa, whoa, slow down here," Charles was muttering, and Ryan felt her hand caught between both of his as he rubbed her fingers, trying to warm her up. "Just back up a minute. I don't know what package you're talking about—"

"Yes, the one you brought. That Marissa got for me when you went shopping for antiques, remember? The one on the bed in Marissa's room just now—"

"No." Charles shook his head. "No, the present I

brought for you is down in the living room. I stuck it under the tree."

"No," Ryan argued, pulling away, making the size of the box with her hands. "The little box—"

"Big box," Charles corrected. "Ryan, I know what she got you. I wrapped it myself, remember? It's a big box. And it's under the tree where I put it. I just saw it—just now—when you ran out of the house—"

Ryan looked at him helplessly. "Then who left that box on the bed for me? Did someone come in the house while everyone was gone?" Her voice rose, working its way toward hysteria. "Charles, her *necklace* was in that box! How could her *necklace* be in that box when she drowned with it? And *where* did that box come from? Oh, my God—"

Her head jerked up as a car pulled into the driveway. She looked at Charles and heard herself whisper, "Oh, no, I can't let Mom see that necklace!"

"Where is it?"

"In Marissa's room—I threw it somewhere on the floor."

She saw Charles run ahead of her into the house . . . she heard her mother and Steve calling to her . . . she watched them as they struggled through the snowdrifts up to the porch.

"Looks like I'll have a lot of shoveling to do." Steve grinned, helping Mrs. McCauley up the steps. "You're out awful early, aren't you? How was the caroling last night? Did you manage to salvage Phoebe's future?"

Mrs. McCauley gave her a weary glance. "I called Phoebe's last night, but you two weren't home yet. I wanted you to know I'd been stranded. Where's Charles? Did you two have a good time?"

For once Ryan was glad her mother wasn't really listening. "It was okay. What's in the box?"

"A plaque." Mrs. McCauley smiled sadly, lifting off the lid so Ryan could see. "Glenda gave it to me as a reminder of Marissa. I'm going right upstairs and hang it in her room."

"No, don't!" Ryan grabbed her mother's arm, and Mrs. McCauley winced.

"Ryan, that hurt. What on earth is wrong with you now?"

"Nothing. Nothing at all." Ryan loosened her grip, but began pulling her mother toward the kitchen, all the while trying to signal Steve with her eyes. "I just want to hear all about your visit, that's all. I'll make us some coffee."

"But we can talk about it as soon as I— Ryan, what is the *matter?*" Mrs. McCauley firmly pushed Ryan's hand from her arm and stared at her daughter. "You look terrible this morning. I bet you and Phoebe didn't get a wink of sleep all night, as usual. Just look at her, Steve. You won't be happy until you *do* get sick, will you, Ryan?"

Steve was looking at her, and as Mrs. McCauley suddenly turned to face him, he managed to twist his face into an instant smile while trying to interpret Ryan's frantic gestures behind her mother's back.

"Honestly, Steve, what are you looking so silly about?" Mrs. McCauley said irritably. "Everyone's acting so peculiar around here this morning. . . ."

"Maybe we *should* have coffee first," Steve said quickly, his smile wavering uncertainly as Ryan glanced up the stairs and back to him again. "I'll help you hang the plaque up later. Uh . . . where's Charles?"

"Still asleep, I think." Ryan stepped aside to let her mother pass, and Steve gave an amused grin.

"Welcome to the asylum, Steve." He looked good-naturedly perplexed. "Well, I'm glad to see nothing's changed much since I was last here. Ryan, would you mind telling me what's going—"

Ryan thought fast. "It's Charles. He's not feeling too well this morning—you know, the party last night and all—well, you know how Mom can be if she found out—"

"Morning everyone. Some storm last night, huh?"

Steve and Ryan glanced up as Charles came down the stairs. Mrs. McCauley peered around the kitchen door and smiled.

"There you are, Charles. Did you have a good time last night?"

"Great, thanks." Charles paused on the bottom step, his eyes brushing casually over Ryan as he even more casually patted one pocket of his jeans. "Nothing like caroling to put you in the Christmas spirit, right, Ryan?"

Ryan gave him a desperate look, her mind spinning. *You found it, didn't you? Tell me you found it—don't tell me I imagined that, too—*

"Well, I think Ryan looks terrible this morning." Mrs. McCauley seemed annoyed. "She's much too pale, and she's got those dark circles under her eyes that always mean she's coming down with something. And how'd you get all these scratches? I think you should lie down, Ryan. Maybe I should call the doctor."

"I don't need a doctor—" Ryan began, but Charles cut her off.

"Good idea. I'll go back up with you, Ryan—I need to get some stuff out of my bag."

Ryan felt Charles's hand close around her elbow, guiding her up to the second floor. *I'm going to explode, I'm going to start screaming, any minute, any second, I'm just going to go completely crazy. . . .* She snapped back to attention as Charles squeezed her arm.

"It's okay, Ryan, I found it. Come on, let's talk."

They were in the hallway now, and Charles was steering her toward Marissa's room.

"No—I don't want to go back in there—"

"We have to. They're less likely to hear us in there."

As the door closed behind them, Ryan perched uneasily on the window seat and watched Charles listen several minutes to make sure that Mom and Steve had really stayed downstairs. Satisfied, he turned to face her and fished into his pocket. Ryan's heart clutched as she recognized the chain dangling from his fingers.

"It's hers," she said shakily.

"Are you sure?" He looked doubtful. "It *looks* like the one she always wore, but that doesn't make any sense."

Ryan began rocking, stiff, jerky movements, her body one giant knot. "This is impossible—you know that, don't you? *Impossible!* She had it on that day—I *saw* her—she was fooling with it. She had it on when she—"

"Are you . . . positive?" Charles asked again quietly, and Ryan nearly screamed at him.

"Of course I am! Don't you think I know what happened that day!" As Charles lowered his eyes, she wrapped her arms around herself and fought for composure. "Okay . . . okay, I'm sorry—but what does this *mean?* Is Marissa still alive? Did *she* put it here? I keep *seeing* her—I don't even know what's *happening* anymore. . . . Charles, *how did this get here?*"

Ryan stopped, her whole body weak and shaking. She felt sick and bent her head, taking deep breaths. When Charles spoke, his voice sounded hollow and distant.

"You know she's not alive. You *know* that. There has to be some explanation. Some logical reason."

"Well, then, what is it?" Ryan gave a nervous laugh, shocked that she could find it even remotely amusing. "If Marissa's really gone . . . then why isn't her necklace with her?"

Chapter 12

Ryan?"

As Mrs. McCauley's voice sounded from the hall-way, Ryan nearly jumped out of her skin. She stared fearfully as Charles opened the door with an easy smile.

"Oh, good, Charles, I'm glad you're here. Maybe *you* can talk some sense into her. Ryan, I *insist* that you lie down. I called Mr. Partini and told him you wouldn't be in today."

"Mom—I—"

"He was very understanding," Mrs. McCauley said firmly. "Now, I want you to rest. Dr. Wilson's calling in a prescription for you—just something to help you relax."

"But I don't need to—"

"You're entirely too high strung." Her mother glanced apologetically at Charles. "She's not usually this bad—she's been under a great strain. She hasn't been herself."

"Can I pick up that prescription for you?" Charles offered. "I'd like to do something to make myself useful."

"I'll go," Steve volunteered. He came up behind Mrs. McCauley and winked at Ryan over her mother's head. "The roads are pretty well cleared off by now, and I need to stop at home for a minute, anyway. Got a little bit of packing to do before my trip." He smiled down at Mrs. McCauley and gave her shoulder a squeeze as her face fell. "Only a couple days! It's *good* I'm going away—you guys will appreciate me so much more when I come back!"

"Oh, I just hate to think of you gone," Mrs. McCauley said sadly. "The house will be so empty.

"You have Ryan," Steve reminded her. "And now you have Charles. Okay, Ryan, get to bed. I'll be back as soon as I can." *And then we'll talk,* his eyes communicated to Ryan.

"Then would you take me to the grocery store, Charles?" Mrs. McCauley motioned Ryan toward the bed and pulled an extra blanket from a closet shelf. "I'm running low on just about everything. Do you mind?"

"My pleasure." Charles gave a sweeping bow. "I hope you feel better, Ryan."

Ryan turned her face away, not looking at the door again until she heard everyone leave. In the heavy quiet she lay motionless, but she could feel her mind slowly and steadily crumbling.

I have to make some sense out of this. . . . I have to talk to somebody—

She grabbed the phone and dialed Phoebe's number. After seven endless rings, she was finally answered by a blast of rock music.

"Jinx!" she tried to shout but barely managed a croak. "Is Phoebe there?"

"What?"

"Turn down the—" Ryan took a deep breath. *Come on, Ryan, get a grip.* . . . "Jinx, turn that down and get Phoebe!"

"She's not here!"

"When will she be back?"

"When she wants to. Get lost, McCauley—I'm not a social director—"

"I'm not kidding, Jinx—it's a matter of life and death!"

"Huh?"

"I said—" Ryan shook so violently that she had to hold the receiver with both hands to keep from dropping it.

"I heard that party last night was wild," Jinx said. "I heard someone spiked the cider."

The cider! So I wasn't drugged after all. . . . *Charles wasn't trying to get rid of me . . . he really did hit the dog . . . he really did leave me there by mistake—*
"Jinx—"

There was a thud as the phone was thrown down, and then the volume of the music took an unexpected plunge.

"Okay." Jinx sighed. "What do you want me to tell her?"

"Tell her I have to talk to her. Tell her I need her to come and get me as soon as she can!"

"You might have a long wait. She and that Michael guy went out early this morning. She *must* be in love to have her eyes open before noon on a Saturday."

"You don't understand how important this is! I *have* to come over there—"

"So fly. Jeez, McCauley, you sound terrible. You have a hangover or what?"

"Can your mom or dad come and get me?"

"They're down at Aunt Agnes's. They won't be back till late tomorrow night."

"Jinx, *please*—"

"Oh, no, you don't. I just took a nice big pizza out of the oven, and I'm *very* comfortable here on the couch."

"I'll pay for your gas."

"With what, your looks? That wouldn't even get me out of my driveway."

Ryan slammed down the phone and sat stiffly on the edge of the bed.

How did that necklace get away from Marissa?

How did it get in the bedroom?

Ryan's head came up, her blood going icy in her veins. *What was that?* For just a second she thought she'd heard something downstairs . . . a door creaking open . . . a footstep . . .

"Steve?"

Ryan went to the top of the stairs and peered down. The house held its breath around her. She went back to Marissa's room and crawled into bed, feeling cold all over.

Someone was in this house . . . someone knew where Marissa's room was . . .

A car door slammed outside, and as someone came in and started up the stairs, Ryan scooted back against the headboard and watched the door with frightened eyes.

"Steve?" she called fearfully.

"No. Me." Jinx poked his head in and scowled. "Don't worry, McCauley, your secret's safe with me."

"What secret? Oh, I'm so glad you're here!" Ryan threw off the covers, and Jinx quickly turned his back. "You don't have to be so polite, Jinx—I'm dressed."

"I'm not being polite. I just didn't want to throw up on the rug when I saw your body."

"I can't believe you came." Ryan slipped up behind him and tried to give him a hug, but he wiggled out of her arms. "I didn't think you really would."

"Yeah, well, that's obvious. So who is he, anyway? I probably know him, right?"

Ryan frowned. "Who?"

"No, that's what *I* asked *you*. Pay attention and try to get it right this time."

"Jinx . . ." Ryan sighed. "What are you talking about?"

"Oh, come on, I've already seen him, so you don't have to play dumb." Jinx snapped his fingers. "Oops, sorry . . . I forgot you weren't playing."

"You're making even less sense than usual," Ryan said, annoyed. "Will you please tell me what you're—"

Jinx sighed. "The guy, McCauley. The boyfriend. The secret admirer. I saw him just now sneaking out the back door, so quit pretending . . ." His words faded as he watched the reaction on her face. "The guy," he said again and tapped Ryan on the forehead. "Hello? Anyone home?"

"What guy?" Ryan whispered.

"I told you, he—" Jinx broke off as Ryan sagged back against the wall.

"You're teasing me, right? Please say you're—"

"He was coming out the back door when I drove up—I could see him through the trees. By the time I hit the driveway, I guess he'd taken off through the woods."

"Oh, Jinx, nobody was here—I mean, nobody I knew about—"

"You mean you've been here alone? You didn't see him?" Jinx was already out in the hall, racing down the stairs. "Stay here—I'll take a look!"

That noise I thought I heard downstairs . . . someone must have been in the house with me. . . . On shaky legs Ryan stood at Marissa's window with its clear view of the backyard. She saw Jinx searching the area, and she saw prints in the snow leading down the slope and into the woods. Jinx looked back toward the house, and she raised the window to call down to him.

"Jinx, come back inside!"

"Want me to see where these footprints go?"

"No! Just please come back in here!"

"Should I call the police?"

"Jinx!"

"Okay, okay, I'm coming."

Ryan went downstairs and was holding the kitchen door when he came back inside.

"Did you see anyone?"

"Not a soul. You sure you weren't expecting anyone?"

"Positive. When you saw this person—"

"Guy," Jinx corrected. "He was a guy."

"Are you *sure* he was coming out of the house?"

"Well, he was on the kitchen steps, with his back to the door. I just figured he was."

"Maybe you scared him off, and he never *got* inside. What'd he look like, could you tell?"

Jinx shook his head. "I wasn't close enough—but he looked pretty big. Hey, you better sit down or something." Dragging her to a chair, he forced her into it, then ran cold water on the dishrag and dabbed clumsily at her face.

"I need to talk to Phoebe," she whispered.

"Not unless your name is Michael. Only Michael's got her attention this weekend."

"Oh, Jinx, please . . . I've got to tell her what's going on. . . ." Ryan closed her eyes wearily. When she opened them again, Jinx was squatting on his heels in front of her.

"Maybe it was a hunter," he said helpfully. "You know how they're always wandering onto your property. Maybe he wanted to use your phone, and you didn't hear him knock."

"No . . . not a hunter . . ." she mumbled, and Jinx tried again.

"A delivery man."

"I didn't order anything. And anyway, where was his car?"

"A delivery man on foot." Jinx rocked back on his heels, holding on to the rungs of her chair for balance. "You look terrible. Even more than usual, I mean."

"I feel terrible. I . . ." Her eyes misted, and she stared down at him, her voice small and frightened. "Jinx . . . do you think I'm crazy?"

She'd expected the usual insults, delivered in the usual quick-fire manner. What she hadn't expected were his hands reaching out to hers, grasping them tightly, and the way his eyes looked suddenly serious and sad.

"Come on, McCauley," he whispered. "Talk to me."

She told him everything—all that had happened, all her fears and suspicions—and the whole time she talked, Jinx never said a word, just crouched there, holding her hands.

"I don't know what to believe anymore," she ended. "I don't know what to think."

Jinx was silent a minute. "You really spent the night with Winchester?"

"Jinx!" Ryan looked indignant. "That hardly seems very important compared to the rest of this mess."

Jinx looked a little embarrassed. "Yeah, okay. You're right. So how come you never told anyone Marissa might be in some kind of trouble?"

"She made me promise not to. At first I thought she was just joking. And then . . ." She caught herself, feeling disloyal.

"Yeah." Jinx nodded. "Some guy."

"But then she was gone, and whatever it was didn't

matter anymore anyway," Ryan said miserably. "And I swore I wouldn't tell. I shouldn't even have told you."

"Ryan, Marissa's dead. I really don't think she'd care."

"But I promised. It was our secret. The last secret we ever shared." Ryan groaned. "I think something terrible is happening. Or going to happen. To me, maybe. I don't want to think that. Talk me out of thinking that."

"Okay. Nothing bad's happening, and nothing bad's gonna happen."

"Promise?"

"Look—" Jinx rubbed his chin and began pacing. "What if everything's just the way it seems?"

"What do you mean?"

"Some kid just messed up the dollhouse. Coincidence. Some fat guy likes to window-shop. Coincidence. Charles really *is* a friend of Marissa's . . . he really *has* just come here out of the goodness of his heart . . . he *wants* to be your friend—" Jinx glanced up. "Obviously, the guy must be *desperate* for friends, but that's his problem." Jinx kept pacing. "He didn't know you got out of the van, and you nearly gave him a heart attack, and Winchester saved your life, and you slept there."

"Jinx"—Ryan shot him a chilly glance that he chose to ignore—"what about the necklace?"

"I'm thinking."

"What about the garage? The body in the car?"

"That door's always jamming, you know that."

"The body," Ryan repeated impatiently. "The ghost in the woods."

"Both times it was dark, right? It could have been shadows—"

"Shadows don't honk. Shadows don't talk."

"Come on, McCauley, you already said you felt weird at the party—"

Ryan gave an exasperated sigh. "I only had one cup of cider!"

"Then it was probably some farmer. He didn't see you, and he was"—Jinx thought quickly—"talking to his buddy. He said, 'I can't come home for Christmas, I'm staying here instead.'"

"No." Ryan thought a moment. "That wasn't it."

"'I can't come home for Christmas . . . I'll be sick in bed.'"

Ryan gave him a scathing look.

"'I can't come home for Christmas . . . I'm Fred.'"

"Fred!"

"Ed?"

"Jinx—"

"Well, you said talk you out of it!" Jinx said crossly. "You're not being very cooperative."

"Don't you understand this is really serious!"

"What's serious is that you spent all night in a cabin with Winchester Stone! That's what's serious."

Ryan stared at him, her anger rising. "He was a perfect gentleman! And anyway, why do *you* care so much about it?"

"I don't," Jinx said quickly, shrugging his shoulders, looking away. "I don't care at all."

"A perfect gentleman," Ryan reiterated. "I trusted him completely."

"Right. This coming from Miss Approachable of Fadiman High. Face it, McCauley, any guy who even *looks* at you is a criminal, as far as you're concerned. You don't trust anything male, and you've got about as much self-confidence as a rabbit. There're lots of guys who'd grab you up if—" Abruptly he broke off, then busied himself at the sink filling a glass of water.

"If what?" Ryan said, embarrassed. "How would you know?"

"Trust me on this one. I know."

"Who, then? Who's interested in me?"

"You wouldn't catch on if they looked you right in the face." Jinx scowled. "Which no one could do and live, 'cause you're so ugly."

"We're way off the subject here—quit being a jerk."

"Well, excuse me! Going over all the ways you're being terrorized just happens to put me in a bad mood, okay?"

"Then . . . you believe me? That someone's after me?"

"I didn't say that. I believe you're paranoid as hell, but what's new?"

"Should we go to the police?"

"With what? All your concrete evidence? The ghosts you've seen? A four-inch tall victim of doll abuse?"

Furious tears filled Ryan's eyes. "It's not funny, Jinx—I'm so scared!"

"Am I laughing?" he challenged her. "Do you see

me laughing at all this, McCauley? I'm just telling you that if you go to the cops with these wild stories of yours, they're really gonna wonder about some things—"

"Like *what* things?"

"Like what you had to drink at that party—and all your problems at school—and where you spent the night last night—"

"But—well—I know it all sounds kind of funny—"

"Right, and that's what the cops'll think, too. Just listen to what you've been telling me! You said yourself Mrs. Corbett had a conference with your mom— they think you should see a shrink!"

"But that's not fair! I'm telling the truth!"

"Okay, then, where's the necklace? Let me see it."

Ryan stared at him. She hung her head and shook it slowly. "I don't have it. I guess Charles still does."

"I rest my case."

"Look, Jinx, someone might have been in the house a little while ago—he could be the one following me all this time!"

"Following you? You've actually *seen* someone following you?"

"Well . . . no . . . I . . ." Her voice sank. "I've just felt it." She raised her eyes again, imploring him. "Oh, Jinx, what am I going to do? You've got to believe me! Say you believe me—*please!*"

"I believe you."

"You're just saying that!"

"Oh, hell . . ." He glanced at her quickly, then

toward the hallway. "You're giving me the creeps, McCauley. Let's get outta here."

"You're the only one I've told," Ryan said, following him downstairs. "I'm not crazy. . . . I'm not imagining things—"

"And I gave up pizza for this," Jinx grumbled. "I gave up pizza and my nice soft couch for this. I gave up pizza and my couch and the football game for—"

"I'll buy you a new pizza. We can stop on the way."

"And gas."

"Yes." Ryan sighed. "And gas. Just let me leave a note."

"Terrific, McCauley. Now they'll come to *my* house and terrorize *me!*"

Ryan felt drained. She sat stiffly in the car and scarcely even realized when they pulled into the service station. She reached into her purse and handed Jinx a wad of bills, watching vacantly as he hopped out to pump gas. A tapping sound startled her, and she looked up to see Winchester's father smiling in at her through the window. She rolled it down, and he leaned partway in.

"How you doing there, little lady? After what you been through last night, you should take it easy."

Ryan couldn't help smiling back. "I wanted to thank you again. I could have died out there."

"Hey, now, no thanks necessary. I'm just glad Winchester was there to help. Hope your folks weren't worried, though, wondering about you."

"No," Ryan fibbed. "They understood about the phone and all."

Mr. Stone fixed her with a puzzled grin. "What about the phone?"

"The storm knocking out the lines," Ryan said. "I hope you got it fixed okay."

"Nothin' to fix." And Winchester's father was shaking his head while something cold snaked up Ryan's spine.

"Oh, I must have misunderstood . . ."

"Must have," Mr. Stone said cheerfully. "Far as I know, that phone worked just fine last night."

Chapter 13

As Jinx slid in and started the car, he eyed her skeptically. "You okay?"

"I just want to sleep, that's all."

"Well, do it in Phoebe's room. I got friends coming over."

"Not those slimy little guys you always hang around with."

"Well, who asked you? Like it's even your house." Jinx took a corner too fast, and the car skidded on some ice.

"If you're not careful, I won't even live long enough to get to your house." *Winchester lied to me . . . and I just said I trusted him. . . .* "Why are we stopping?"

Jinx looked at her in amazement. "I swear, McCauley, you've got a brain like a slug. Pizza. Remember?"

He held out his hand, and Ryan dug through her wallet for more money. Not finding any, she searched through her purse, then emptied the contents on her lap.

"Terrific," Jinx grumbled. "So I starve."

"Oh, just wait a minute," Ryan grumbled back.

"The lining's loose on the bottom—sometimes I find all kinds of money under there." As she pulled out a twenty, her look of triumph turned to surprise. "Look —some film!"

"Big deal. Declare a holiday."

"No . . ." Ryan shook her head. "No, I remember —Marissa gave this to me. The day of the accident. God . . . it's been buried under here all this time. . . ."

"With your brain. Come *on*, I'm hungry—"

"Oh, Jinx, can we stop and drop this off at the drugstore? Please—"

"Yeah, yeah, just give me the money before I'm too weak to walk!" He disappeared into the building, and Ryan leaned back with a groan.

Maybe he didn't know about the phone—you really want to believe that, don't you, because he was so nice and—

Someone's watching me.

Ryan jerked upright, her hands slamming flat against her window. She could see the whole parking lot and the street beyond, but there weren't any people anywhere. *Come on, Jinx, hurry up. . . .*

Taking a deep breath, Ryan started to sit back.

She never saw the shadow beside her door. The huge thud on the glass rocked the car, and as she screamed, the black ski mask stared in at her, filling the window.

She saw the door shake as the handle moved and held—

My God, he's trying to get in—

She threw herself across the seat, falling out onto the slippery pavement. She tried to stand up, but she couldn't get a foothold. Panic-stricken, she looked back over her shoulder.

He was coming around the car after her.

As Ryan scrambled up at last, she saw Jinx coming out of the building, and she screamed again as the bulky figure closed the distance behind her.

"Jinx! Help me!"

Ryan saw the pizza box fly into the air as Jinx hurtled toward her attacker. There was a hoarse cry and a thud as Jinx and the man went down together on the ground.

"Run, Ryan!" Jinx yelled. "Get inside! Hurry—call the—"

"Hey, buddy, will you wait a minute? *Wait a minute!*" The voice from the ski mask was muffled, yet instead of sounding dangerous, it only sounded annoyed. "Get off me, will you? What are you, crazy?"

As Jinx gaped at him, his opponent groaned and gave Jinx a shove. Jinx promptly landed in the snow.

"Don't try anything," he said angrily.

"Hey, don't worry"—the stranger held up his hands—"I'm just trying to get up!"

And as the large man finally stumbled to his feet, he worked off the ski mask.

Ryan had never seen him before, but he looked totally unthreatening and totally put out.

"Hey, buddy, I appreciate you trying to defend your

little girlfriend here—I really do—but I just want you to move your car, okay?"

Jinx's mouth fell open. "You . . . want—"

"Your car." The man sighed. "Look, I got deliveries to make. You got me blocked in!"

As one, Ryan and Jinx turned their heads. Now they could see the pizza delivery truck idling in a little alleyway that Jinx's car had barricaded.

Ryan gulped. Jinx closed his eyes for a long moment, as if gathering every ounce of control.

"I'm really sorry," Jinx mumbled, starting forward, but the man shook his head and backed away.

"Hey, pal, forget about it. As a matter of fact, I admire your nerve. I mean, look at you! Look at *me!*" He patted his wide stomach. "I coulda squashed you like a bug!"

Again Jinx closed his eyes. Ryan could see him taking deep breaths. She hurried back to the car and got in, careful to look straight ahead as he finally slid in beside her.

"Jinx—"

"Don't look at me, McCauley."

"I'm not. I just wanted—"

"Don't talk to me, either. You've ruined my day. You've ruined my weekend."

"But see? You were ready to help me, so that proves you *must* believe some of what I told you back at the house—"

"You're ruining my life."

"What about the . . . pizza?"

In answer Jinx hit the accelerator and aimed his car for the take-out box upside down in the snow. She heard a soft crunch as they ran over it.

"Can we still leave the film?" she asked timidly.

"Only if I can leave you with it."

Jinx did stop at the drugstore but stayed silent all the way home. Ryan went straight to Phoebe's room to lie down, and when she woke up, it was nearly eleven. She found Jinx asleep on the couch in the den, the TV blaring away, and she stood there a long time watching him. She was the one who had given him his nickname when they were little—Jinx instead of Jimmy—because, as she'd explained to an agreeable Phoebe, something bad always happened when he was around. Now, however, he didn't look so little anymore, and Ryan was surprised at the changes she'd never noticed till now. The baby face had grown more angular and strong, somehow, and she could see the curve of muscles beneath his sleeves. No wonder girls are calling him, she thought with a small shock. She reached out and gently touched his hair, knowing he'd either kill her or die of embarrassment if he ever found out. When he stirred slightly, she made a quick retreat to the kitchen and was just sitting down to eat something when Phoebe came home, wearing a familiarly dreamy expression.

"Don't tell me," Ryan greeted her. "You're in love."

"To my deepest depths. To my innermost soul." Phoebe pressed her hands to her heart. "This is it, Ryan. This is the big one."

"They're all big ones," Ryan reminded her. "And even bigger ones when they end."

"Oh, but this one won't." Phoebe draped her scarf over her shoulders and shimmied. "He can't resist me."

"Phoebe"—Ryan sighed—"no one can resist you."

"I guess I was born that way."

"I guess."

"So how's your life since I saw you last?"

Ryan stared at her. It seemed like months since she and Phoebe had talked, but now, with the chance right in front of her, Ryan didn't even know where to begin.

Phoebe clapped her hands. "Let's go get cappuccinos at the Coffeehouse!"

"Phoebe, I really don't feel like—"

"It's only eight blocks—we can walk—"

"No, I'm exhausted. All day I've felt like I'm catching a bad cold."

"We *have* to walk. When Dad saw the scratches on the van, he blew a fuse. I can't drive for a week. And I can't tell him Charles did it, 'cause he said no one could drive it but me."

"Why didn't you say something?"

"'Cause I wanted Michael to bring me home. Where's Jinx?"

"Asleep."

"Great. Then we'll take *his* car."

"Phoebe—"

"Dad said I couldn't drive *my* car—he didn't say anything about Jinx's."

"Jinx will kill you."

"He won't know! By the time he wakes up, we'll be gone!"

"We still have to come back sometime."

"I'll tell him *you* drove!"

Ryan groaned and felt herself being pulled out the door. "That's probably the *worst* thing you could tell him tonight."

The Coffeehouse was noisy and crowded, but they managed to find a booth in back. After ordering, Phoebe proceeded to tell Ryan all about her day with Michael Kilmer, including the three future dates they'd scheduled before he brought her home tonight. She didn't seem to notice that Ryan wasn't listening.

"So I'm going to the dance!" she finished triumphantly. "And you are, too."

"I am?" The stifling heat was making it hard for Ryan to concentrate. *Jinx is right . . . everything is just a coincidence . . . but what about the necklace . . . ?*

"With Charles Eastman."

"What!" Coffee spewed out of Ryan's mouth, and Phoebe hurriedly grabbed a napkin and dabbed at Ryan's chin. "Have you totally lost your—"

"I had a feeling you'd take it like this," Phoebe fussed, creasing her napkin primly, folding her arms on the tabletop.

"I don't even want to discuss this," Ryan said.

"Maybe my timing is all wrong—"

"Phoebe, you *have* no timing."

"Oh, Ryan, *please*—just ask him?"

"No."

"I want us to go to the dance together. We'd have such a wonderful time!"

"No."

"I know he'd take you if you asked him! Your mom thinks so, too—"

"My mom? You asked my mom?"

"Well, when Michael and I stopped at your house to pick up the van, I just mentioned—"

"Oh, God, Phoebe, you didn't mention it to Charles—"

"Not exactly. But your mom thinks it'd be good for you to go. I know Charles would think so, too."

"Phoebe, you make me sound like a charity case! Don't you understand? I just can't think about the dance at this particular time of my life." *I'm too busy thinking about coincidences. . . .*

"Oh, Ryan, you're just shy. I bet deep down you're just the tiniest bit interested in him—"

"No, I'm not."

"Well, will you at least think about it?"

"No. Phoebe, leave me alone. I don't want to talk about the dance or Charles Eastman anymore."

"Oh, Ryan, you're breaking my heart." Phoebe looked miserably down at the table. "I was counting on us going together. You're really and truly breaking my heart—it's our absolute *last* New Year's dance together. . . ."

"Phoebe, you'll be having such a fantastic time with Michael, you won't even miss me."

"Yes, I will."

"No, you won't. I promise you won't."

"Yes, I will. Pleeeeeeease?"

"No! And that's final!" *Thank God I didn't tell her—she'd never take me seriously—*

"Well, then, we might as well just go home, I'm so sad now." Phoebe gave Ryan her most pitiful look. "I don't know what you're in such a bad mood about anyway."

They walked back to the car without talking. The streets were empty, except for one Santa Claus standing on a corner, slowly ringing a bell.

"Isn't it a little late for him to be out?" Phoebe nudged Ryan, laughing, then suddenly stopped and let out a groan.

"Oh, my God! Jinx'll have a stroke!"

Frowning, Ryan knelt and examined the front tire. "It looks like someone cut it. Look—*all* the tires are slashed."

"Dammit, who would do such a mean thing! And all the stores are closed!"

Ryan looked down the street and shivered. The Santa Claus had disappeared. "I don't have my key to the toy shop with me, either. Come on, we can call from the Coffeehouse."

Returning to the restaurant, the girls found someone already using the phone, and as the minutes dragged by, Phoebe grew impatient.

"I could have been to the gas station and back again by now," she fretted. "Look, they're getting ready to close—"

"Let's just go, then."

"No—I'll go. It's my fault we're in this mess. You stay here where it's warm and wait for me."

"Phoebe, don't be silly, I'm not letting you go alone."

"You're the one who's getting sick." Phoebe shook her finger under Ryan's runny nose. "You stay here and get us coffee to go, and I'll try to find another phone."

"I think the drugstore has a payphone—try there."

"It's probably quicker if I just walk to the station myself," Phoebe grumbled, digging in her purse. "You got change?"

"What is it with your family? I'm always handing out money."

"I'll be back in a second. You stay warm. If they run you out, just stand under the awning—at least you won't feel the wind."

"Yes, Mother." Ryan watched Phoebe disappear around the corner, then she ordered their drinks and waited.

She waited a long time.

As the restaurant began to empty, Ryan wondered what was taking Phoebe so long. She could feel the coffee getting cold in her sack. She drank one, but when Phoebe still didn't reappear, she drank the other. *I bet that dumb phone wasn't working. . . . I bet she had to walk to the station after all.*

Frowning, Ryan stepped outside and looked up the

street. It was starting to snow again, and she tried to ignore the growing fear in her heart. *She's stopped to talk to someone . . . typical Phoebe, she's forgotten all about me and Jinx's car. . . .*

Thrusting her hands into her pockets, Ryan started up the street, averting her eyes from the alleyways she had to pass. She tried to imagine Phoebe safe in the gas station. She glanced up through a flitter of snow and stopped and stared.

At first she thought she'd imagined it, the Santa Claus standing there ahead of her on the corner. He looked like the one they'd seen near the car—huge and jolly in his fur-trimmed suit—and Christmas lights twinkling from a nearby window sparkled off his heavy black boots. He was stamping his feet as if he was cold, his curly white beard flowing down over his chest.

He was ringing a bell.

Ryan stood there, strangely mesmerized by the magical Santa in the dead of night.

And then she began walking.

He was ringing the bell in time to her footsteps.

She walked faster.

The bell went faster, too, echoing each stab of fear in her heart.

Phoebe . . . I've got to find Phoebe. . . .

Through the softly sprinkling snow Ryan saw Santa standing there on the corner—*just standing there*—like one of Mr. Partini's mechanical dolls, arm up, arm down, ringing, ringing, just standing there, waiting for her to pass—

She swung wide out into the street, rushing away from him up the sidewalk—

Behind her she heard the bell clang as it fell into the snow.

She heard the footsteps coming after her.

"Help, somebody! Please help me!"

The buildings loomed lifelessly around her. As she turned the next corner, she cast a wild glance over her shoulder.

He was plodding through the snow, his head down, unhurried. Ryan could see his boots lifting in long, crushing strides. Without warning she suddenly slipped and fell, and the footsteps began to run.

Oh, no . . . oh, God . . . As Ryan struggled to her hands and knees, her eyes made a terrified sweep of the street—

But now it was empty.

Chapter 14

Ryan!" a voice shouted. "Ryan—what are you doing!"

As Ryan got to her feet, dazed, she saw the tow truck coming toward her with Phoebe hanging out one window.

"Ryan, I told you to wait for me! What happened?"

Ryan stepped back as the truck pulled up beside her, as Mr. Stone leaned out the other side with a grin.

"You must really like being out in the cold, little lady," he teased.

Phoebe opened her door impatiently. "For heaven's sake, Ryan, get in here. What were you doing down on all fours in the snow?"

"I fell," Ryan mumbled. "Santa Claus."

"No, it's Phoebe." Phoebe regarded her friend apprehensively. "Oh, Mr. Stone, I think she's delirious!"

"Stop it, Phoebe, I know who you are, I'm not delirious," Ryan said sharply. "Didn't you see him? He was chasing me—"

"Santa Claus was chasing you?"

"You *must* have seen him—"

"We didn't see anyone," Mr. Stone said. "Lucky for you I came along when I did. Come on—hop in."

"Did you get mugged?" Phoebe asked worriedly, and Mr. Stone looked disgusted.

"You mean, now they're even dressing up like Santa Claus? What if some little kids had seen that—that's terrible!"

"Should we call the police?" Phoebe asked.

"I doubt they'd do anything about it." Mr. Stone sighed. "That mugger's long gone by now."

"But it wasn't a mugger," Ryan protested. "Look— I've still got my purse."

"Well, I musta scared him off." Mr. Stone motioned her to close the door. "You girls better stay at the station, and I'll go take a look at that car of yours."

The girls drank hot chocolate while they waited for Mr. Stone to get back. Ryan was trying to pay attention to the night clerk's fourth boring story when she felt Phoebe nudge her and saw Winchester come through the door. He looked tired, Ryan thought, and he glanced away as he recognized her.

"You need some help?" he asked softly, but it was Phoebe he spoke to, not Ryan.

Phoebe promptly bestowed him a dimpled smile. "Well, actually, we have four flat tires, but your father went to fix them." When he nodded and started to walk away, she nudged Ryan again and added, "He said we could stay here and wait."

"Sure. Make yourself comfortable."

"I'm Phoebe." Phoebe held out her hand, and after an awkward pause Winchester shook it. "You probably know my brother, Jinx? And this is my friend Ryan."

His eyes swept over Ryan but didn't stop. "We've met."

"Oh, that's right." Phoebe's smile widened. "You went out with Marissa, didn't you?"

Oh, Phoebe, stop. Ryan looked down at the floor, at Winchester's black workboots dripping over the old linoleum. *Why did he lie to me about the phone . . . ?*

"My friend Ryan got mugged," Phoebe said proudly.

"Phoebe!" Ryan hissed.

"Right down the street. Your father probably saved her life."

"Did he?" At last Winchester's eyes settled on Ryan's face. Ryan tried to step on Phoebe's toe, but Phoebe slyly moved her foot away.

"Yes, it was terrible. Somebody chased her, but then your father came. Oh, look, there he is now." Phoebe waved out the window as the tow truck pulled in, dragging Jinx's car behind. "So I guess this means I'll have to leave the car, right? Could you keep this kind of quiet? Till I think of something to tell my brother?"

Before Winchester could answer, Mr. Stone came in, and Phoebe went over to talk to him, leaving Ryan standing there.

Winchester poured some coffee . . . raised the cup to his lips, squinting through the steam. "So . . . you're okay."

Ryan nodded. Behind her Mr. Stone told Winchester to take the girls home. Ryan stepped forward and blocked his way.

"You lied about the phone," she said quietly. She watched his face, and the surprise it registered. "Your father said it was working."

"Not when I tried it." He frowned and lowered his eyes. "Maybe one of the kids did it . . . took it off upstairs, and I didn't know."

He looked down for a long time. She could see him swallowing . . . she could see a muscle clench in his jaw.

"I'm sorry if you think I lied to you," he whispered. "But I'm not sorry you stayed."

This time his eyes met hers, holding them, and something fluttered in her chest as he took a step toward her.

"Winchester," Mr. Stone said, "come on now, and get these ladies home—we got work to do."

The three of them rode to Phoebe's in a tow truck, Ryan trapped in the middle. There wasn't much room in the front seat, and again she was all too aware of Winchester's body against hers. She could feel his eyes upon her as she got out, and once inside the house she felt curiously weak.

Phoebe peered cautiously into the kitchen and made a face. "Oh, *damn*—Jinx is on the phone, and I think he's talking to Mom and Dad." She glanced again and looked worried. "What am I going to tell him about his car? I'll have to tell him you—" She broke off as Jinx swung around the doorframe and blocked her path.

"You're dead." Jinx looked decidedly smug. "Dad wants to talk to you."

"Dad?" Phoebe's voice quivered. "Dad's on the phone?"

"Yeah. He called right after the garage did."

"The garage? You mean that stupid night clerk?"

"You really screwed up this time, Phoebe. You know you're grounded, and you're *never* supposed to touch my car unless it's an emergency."

"You told Dad?" Phoebe was shocked. "You actually *told* him? I don't believe it—"

"Get in there." Jinx jerked his thumb toward the kitchen. "He's really mad. You are in *deep* trouble."

"You jerk!" Phoebe sounded tearful. "I can't believe you *told* him—I would have paid for your stupid car—"

"He's grounding you for good this time." Jinx leaned back, looking pleased with himself. "He says no New Year's dance."

Even Ryan looked shocked. As Phoebe stared at Jinx, the silence seemed to grow and grow until the room was unbearable.

"No . . ." Phoebe mumbled. "He wouldn't . . ."

"Think again," Jinx said. "You shouldn't have tried to be so sneaky."

Phoebe disappeared into the kitchen. Ryan could hear her babbling, then pleading, and finally the crash as the receiver came down.

"I *hate* you!" Phoebe came into the hallway and went for Jinx, but he managed to make it to the stairs. "You've ruined my *life!* You've absolutely ruined my *life!* I can't believe you *did* this to me!"

"Hey, *I* didn't do it," Jinx said, his voice rising. He looked indignant but took another step away from her. "You *knew* better—don't blame *me!*"

"This is the most horrible thing you've ever done!" Phoebe was crying now, and as Ryan reached for her, Phoebe pushed her away.

"Well, what am *I* gonna do for a car now, huh?" Jinx threw back. "They didn't just slash my tires— they ripped out half the *insides!* What am *I* gonna do about getting to the dance!"

"Who *cares* about your stupid car?" Phoebe screamed at him. "Why don't you just ask Ryan to go with you like you've *wanted* to do all along, and maybe *she* can drive you!"

Ryan stared from Phoebe to Jinx. Jinx had taken another step back, but his face looked peculiarly drained of color.

"Oh, right"—his laugh sounded forced—"like I'd trust her with my life—"

"Oh, stop it, Jinx, just why not let her hear it? I'm sure she'll be so *flattered* that the jerkiest little guy in the whole *town* has had a *crush* on her his whole *life!*"

Ryan's mouth dropped open, and she stared at Jinx. His face was still pale, but his look had gone defiant. He gave her a grim smile and started up the stairs.

"Yeah, stupid, in her dreams . . ."

"Okay, then, why don't we tell her about the *pictures* you've got, huh? In that box with all your most private stuff?"

Jinx froze. He whirled round and slowly began shaking his head.

"You're crazy, Phoebe. You don't know anything about my stuff—"

"Like hell I don't! That box you keep in your closet—and all those pictures of Ryan—from the time she was little all the way up till now—and what about that *letter* you wrote her but you never mailed —how did it go? 'It's so hard for me to tell you what I'm feeling, because I think you're so—'"

"Shut up, Phoebe!"

"Oh, you don't like it, do you, when *you're* the one who's unhappy." Phoebe gave him her most superior big-sister sneer. "And what else did it say—'I'd love for us to be alone together sometime and—'"

"Phoebe . . ." Jinx's voice had dropped. He was still shaking his head, but the paleness had turned into a creeping, helpless red. "Don't . . ." he whispered.

"And I love the part that—"

"Phoebe, stop it!" Ryan said. As her friend looked at her in surprise, Ryan started toward her, but Phoebe gave a sob and ran past Jinx up to her room. Ryan heard the door slam. She lifted her eyes reluctantly to Jinx, but he was staring at the floor and wouldn't look at her.

"Oh, there she goes again. . . ." Ryan laughed, a phony, nervous sound. "Don't pay any attention to her—*I* never do when she does that to me. She's so upset, she doesn't even know what she's saying—you know how she gets—"

Flustered, Ryan broke off. Jinx hadn't moved, and she could hear Phoebe wailing upstairs.

"Wow, look at the time!" Ryan exclaimed. "I better call Mom to come and get me!"

After escaping into the kitchen, she dialed her number with shaking hands. *Oh, Phoebe, what have you done—*

"Steve? Can you pick me up? I'm at Phoebe's—"

"Hey, kiddo, what's the matter? You crying?"

"It's just . . . Jinx and Phoebe had a fight."

"With you caught in the middle?"

"You could say that. Please hurry."

Ryan didn't have long to wait. As they drove away from the house, she looked up and saw Jinx watching from his window. She waved, but the curtains fell shut.

"Well, you can stop worrying about Charles Eastman," Steve told her. "Looks like all his intentions are as noble as he said they were. 'A' student. And now I know where I thought I'd heard his name—he's assistant editor of the paper—*very* well respected."

Ryan scarcely heard him. She could still see Jinx frozen on the stairs . . . the look on his face . . .

"What's wrong?" Steve asked kindly. "You look beat. And your mom's not too happy about you flying the coop. Just a friendly warning." He winked at her.

"So what else is new?" Ryan sighed. "I wish things could just be normal again."

"Me, too, Ryan."

There was a long moment of silence. Ryan forced a smile.

"So what about that important interview? You been practicing?"

Steve gave an exaggerated grimace. "Department chair—pretty scary, huh?"

"Probably not as scary as the interview will be. Once that's over, piece of cake." Ryan patted his arm. "You'll get the job. We all know you will. Mom's going to be so proud."

"Well, I don't have it yet, so recruit some finger-crossers for me, will you?"

"You got it. So when do you leave?"

"Tomorrow night. I hate going at a time like this, but at least Charles is here to help out."

I hate you leaving, too, because it's Christmas, because I'm so unhappy, because you're fun to have around, because . . . because everything—

"Ryan," Steve broke into her thoughts. "Your mom really loves you, you know."

Ryan said nothing. A dozen emotions choked her, and she stared out the window.

"She does," Steve said again. "Even though I know she doesn't show it much these days."

Ryan had a hazy image of her mother's face, superimposed with Marissa's . . . and then without warning, Jinx's expression came again, hurt and embarrassed and helpless—and she shoved it away.

"So what was Mom doing when you left?"

"Sleeping. I don't know where Charles was. Last I

heard, he'd taken the car over to get gas. And by the way, he might not be so bad to have around after all," Steve teased. "I've already got him shoveling snow!"

He let Ryan off and she tiptoed upstairs, thankful to be alone with her thoughts at last. There were so many confused emotions whirling through her brain that she felt numb, and as she let herself into Marissa's room, it didn't register right away that the bedside lamp was already on, that the closet was open, that a tall shadow was leaning over the desk . . .

And as Charles Eastman turned and looked straight at her, Ryan saw the knife in his hand, aimed at the lock on one desk drawer.

Chapter 15

What are you doing!"

As Ryan burst into the room, something went across Charles's face—some fleeting emotion that Ryan couldn't identify—that melted immediately into a sheepish smile.

"God, Ryan, I didn't hear you come home!"

"What are you— Get away from there!"

"Well . . . sure. Hey, I didn't mean any—"

"You don't have *any* right to be in here. When Mom finds out about this—"

"There's no need to tell her." Charles backed away. "You wouldn't want to upset her, and I didn't hurt anything."

"How dare you come in here!"

Charles nodded contritely as he tucked the knife into his belt. "I guess I did get a little carried away. But if you'd just listen and let me explain—"

"Start explaining. And while you're at it, where's the necklace?"

In answer, Charles reached into one pocket and dangled the chain between his fingers. Ryan took it from him slowly, staring down at it in her open palm.

"It *is* hers, I know it. What's going on, Charles?"

When he didn't answer, she looked up at him. His eyes looked worried, and he sank down onto the end of the bed.

"I didn't want to tell you, Ryan. I didn't want you to worry after everything you've been through. But I'm going crazy keeping it to myself . . . and you've got a right to know."

Ryan stared at him, her whole body going cold. "My God," she whispered. "Charles . . . what is it?"

"How strong are you, Ryan?" Charles asked tightly. "I mean, really—how strong?"

Something in his tone alarmed her, and she put one hand to her throat. "What do you mean—what—"

"The necklace." He gave a curt nod. "I haven't been able to quit thinking about it—or about something else that happened at school about a month ago."

"Marissa?" Ryan murmured.

He paused, as if searching for words, then went on slowly. "She and I worked on the paper together; she had the gossip column. Marissa loved her job, and she was good at it—enthusiastic . . . talented at sniffing out rumors. Right before Thanksgiving she started acting . . . I don't know . . . preoccupied. Distracted. Like she was bothered about something. Or . . . scared."

Ryan looked at him in surprise. "That's how she acted with me, too—she seemed different from the minute she got home from school."

"She told me she was pretty sure she'd uncovered something big," Charles said solemnly. "She said it was an accident, that she'd just stumbled onto it, but that it was real scandal material if she could prove anything."

"She didn't say what it was?"

Charles shook his head. "It was weird—she seemed half excited about it, half terrified."

Ryan let out a long sigh and sat on the window seat, facing him. She put the necklace on the cushion beside her.

"She told me she was in trouble." Ryan gulped. "Maybe even serious. That last day we were together —she was so nervous and jumpy, and she kept saying she didn't want to go into it, but maybe she'd know something when she got back to school."

"That's what she told me, too!" Charles leaned forward eagerly. "She said she had some evidence— that she was taking it home with her and—"

"Oh, my God!" Ryan jumped up, her hands to her mouth.

"Ryan, what's the—"

"Oh, my God, Charles—the *film!* Marissa wanted me to drop off some film that day. She needed to take the pictures back to school with her! Do you think—"

"Film . . ." Charles was staring at her, his mouth open, his head shaking in amazement. "Then there really *was* something. . . . So this film . . . you still have it?"

"Yes! I mean, no! I mean, I forgot about it till today! I dropped it off this afternoon!"

"Where? You're sure the film was hers?"

"Yes! Yes! At the drugstore—only they were closing —they said it'd be ready Monday morning—"

"Because tomorrow's Sunday." Charles groaned. He shook his head and then, to Ryan's surprise, reached for her hand. "Ryan, do you realize what this means?"

Her voice was shaking so that she could hardly speak. "That . . . that Marissa might have been . . ."

She couldn't say the word. She closed her eyes and leaned against him.

"If she really *was* on to some scandal," Charles said gravely, "and if someone knew about that film, they could have followed her. They could have been following her for a long time, waiting to get her alone—"

"She said someone tailed her home from school"— Ryan's voice was trembling—"but I never dreamed . . ."

Charles looked pale. He jumped up and thrust his hands into his pockets. "If someone brought that necklace here, then that someone—"

"Must be the . . . killer," Ryan finished.

Charles avoided her eyes. "Maybe he doesn't know how much *you* know about it, Ryan. How much you saw that day."

"Then that means someone really is after me." Her eyes widened and her voice came out the faintest whisper. "If someone murdered Marissa . . . oh, Charles—are they going to kill me, too?"

Chapter 16

Charles offered to drive Ryan to work the next day, and she eagerly accepted.

"I didn't sleep a wink," she told him as they came into town. "I had bad dreams all night."

"Me, too," Charles admitted. "It seems so—so—impossible! We were jumping to an awful lot of conclusions last night. It's not like we have any proof, either. We can't very well go to the police and say anything. At least, not without those pictures."

Ryan looked troubled. "I thought about that, too. But how else can you explain the necklace unless someone took it from her?"

"I can't." Charles shrugged, glancing over at her. "I guess someone could have picked it up later in the woods. Maybe she dropped it before she fell."

"But then whoever found it had to have known it was hers. In order to give it back, I mean."

"Maybe someone saw her fall through the ice." Charles thought a moment. "Maybe they didn't have anything to do with it, but they saw it happen."

"I'd rather believe that than think someone's after me."

"Why do you keep saying that? I wish you'd stop—"

"Sometimes"—Ryan ducked her head—"I really think I *am* going crazy."

Charles lapsed into silence, and as he pulled up near the toyshop, Ryan forced a smile in his direction.

"Do you want to come in? Just don't mind Mr. Partini. When he sees you, he'll probably make a fuss."

No sooner had they stepped inside, than Ryan's prediction came true.

"Ah, *Bambalina*, you surprise me! Here I think you feel sick, and all the time you be *love*sick, eh? With this new fella of yours?"

Ryan made a helpless gesture to Charles, who seemed amused by the whole thing. "He's just a friend, Mr. Partini. He was a friend of my— Oh, never mind. But I really didn't feel well yesterday," she said.

"And I believe you!" The old man nodded in exaggerated seriousness and patted her shoulder. "I *like* this fella—"

"Mr. Partini—"

"You bring him anytime! Anytime!"

"But Mr. Partini, he's not—"

"You bad girl, hiding him from me, Ryan." He shook his finger, then caught Ryan in a hug. "But I'm so happy for you, I gonna forgive you, eh?"

Ryan could hardly stand to look at Charles, but Charles only winked. After a personal tour of the toyshop, he took off, leaving Ryan to spend her busiest Sunday ever.

By five o'clock Ryan was exhausted and eager to go home. As she waited for her mother's car, she heard the phone ring in the back of the shop, and after a brief conversation, Mr. Partini appeared behind her in the doorway.

"Your mother's gonna be late, *Bambalina*. She says for you to meet her on the corner in half an hour, eh?"

Ryan nodded and saw the way he tried to glance discreetly at the clock. "It's all right, Mr. Partini, I know you have some toys to deliver tonight. Why don't you go on—I'll lock up."

"Oh, you caught me looking! Is okay? You don't mind?" He looked so grateful that Ryan smiled.

"Of course not. I'll see you tomorrow."

He patted her cheek with one soft hand. "You a good girl, Ryan—what would I do without you? And hey"—he winked—"that's one cute fella!"

He shuffled back to the workshop, and Ryan heard him lock the door as he left. Minutes later his old car chugged off into the darkness, and silence settled softly over the shop.

Ryan leaned against the wall and tried to think. Her mind had been in such a turmoil that she'd finally resigned herself to a perpetual headache. *Marissa . . . the necklace . . . the film . . . Am I in danger or just caught up in coincidences? Charles . . . Winchester . . . Jinx*— her cheeks flamed, even though she'd tried so hard not to think about last night. *I don't know what to feel about anything anymore*—

Suddenly her mind went blank. She was staring at the front of the store, and something was staring back in at the window—someone—in a lumpy coat and ski mask—huge gloves cupped around black knit eyeholes . . . the head rotating slowly from side to side . . .

Ryan's breath caught in her throat. Very slowly she flattened herself against the wall and tried to slide down onto the floor. Because of her position, the stranger hadn't seen her yet, but she knew it was only a matter of seconds . . .

She huddled there, scarcely daring to breathe, and tried to draw back into the shadows. She didn't have to see the eyes to know they were making a slow, careful sweep of the shop. She could *feel* them.

They were frighteningly cold.

She saw the head tilt slightly, as if thinking. She heard feet scraping pavement . . .

The doorknob began to turn . . .

Oh, my God, I forgot to lock it!

As the front door groaned slowly inward, the bell tinkled spookily overhead, and Ryan slid along the wall and underneath a desk. Icy trickles of sweat chilled her, and she wrapped her arms around herself to keep from shaking.

The silence went on . . . on . . .

And then the feet began to move. Slow, deliberate steps upon the creaking floorboards.

They passed right beside her hiding place.

Terrified, she saw his boots, not ten inches from where she crouched.

And then the voice came . . .

One she knew . . .

"Hi, this is Marissa . . ." And it *was* Marissa, *her* voice—real and laughing, fuzzy and faraway—"but I'm not here . . ."

"Marissa," Ryan whimpered, and she clapped her hand over her mouth, not sure if she'd spoken aloud or only in her fear-crazed mind—

The footsteps stopped.

He can hear me, I know he can, he must be able to—

And then . . . in the deathly quiet . . . the trains started up . . . slowly at first . . . then faster . . . faster . . . little engines chugging . . . tiny whistles blowing . . . around and around—

From some forgotten corner a baby doll cried in a tinny, mournful wail—"Ma . . . ma . . . ma . . . ma . . ."

The mechanical Santa Claus burst into insane laughter.

Ryan could see the wild eyes of the carousel horses—nostrils flaring—*My God, they're alive, they're moving, I can't get out—*

Sick with terror, Ryan clamped her hands over her ears and curled herself into a ball. They were coming closer now, all the toys . . . skates crashing into the wall . . . a top spinning crazily past the desk . . .

If I try for the door, maybe I can make it—maybe he won't hear me—

Ryan took a deep breath and ran.

She never expected the door to be jammed.

Oh, God—something's wrong with the lock—

As she frantically twisted the handle, she cast a desperate look back over her shoulder. *Is that him—moving in the corner? By the dollhouse? Near the tree?* She couldn't see anything now—just black, murky shadows—but he seemed to be everywhere—*everywhere*—and *nowhere*—the trains faster and faster—the Santa laughing and laughing—

Without warning the elves started singing their Christmas carols . . . but on low speed, demons' voices . . .

"Help! Let me out!"

She hammered on the glass and screamed, trying to shut out the unearthly sound of Marissa's voice—*"I'm not here . . . I'm not here—"*

The tree lights blinked on.

A baby carriage started rolling toward her across the floor.

Glass shattered as Ryan's fists went through. Her hands were slippery on the latch, and as it finally gave, she stumbled out onto the sidewalk.

She never looked back . . .

Just raced widly toward the corner, leaving a trail of blood behind her in the snow.

Chapter 17

Her mother wasn't waiting for her.

As Ryan looked frantically up and down the empty sidewalks, she thought she heard the bell over the toy shop door.

"No—no—"

She felt as if she were trapped in a recurring nightmare—running once again through the dark streets, snow clouds covering the stars. The only light came from a few sputtering streetlamps and the sign in the Coffeehouse window—CLOSED.

If I can just get to the gas station—Winchester—how many more blocks? Four? Five? She began to think she'd gone the wrong way when she suddenly saw it up ahead—the pumps, the group of boys hanging around the garage—

"Jinx!" she gasped. She saw the faces turn toward her as one, Jinx looking up from under the hood of a car, his cheeks stained with dirt.

"Get outta here," he said gruffly. "Don't you ever get tired of chasing after me?"

She heard the snickers around him, and she saw him

start to grin, but as she stepped forward into the light, everyone seemed to freeze.

"Jinx—" she began, and *why is he looking at me that way, why are they all staring at me like that*—

"Somebody call the cops," one of them said, and for the first time Ryan looked down.

There was blood everywhere.

She didn't have a jacket on, and there was blood on her sleeves, on her white sweater, on her jeans. Blood was running down her wrists, and there were dark red spatters around her feet.

"Holy sh—" Jinx came around the car. "Does somebody have a rag? Quick, someone, bring me a rag!"

"You better get her to a doctor or something," someone else spoke up, and Ryan realized they all sounded so scared, as scared as she suddenly felt—

"I . . . I did this," she said stupidly, holding up her hands, and as the boys exchanged wary looks, Jinx was suddenly grabbing her arms, binding them together in a towel.

"God, McCauley," he murmured, "get in the car."

She felt him shoving her into a front seat, heard him slamming a door—

"You've got to go back there!" Ryan told him. "I left the door open—Mr. Partini trusted me—"

"What are you *talking* about?"

"The toyshop! The toys were after me, but *he* was there—*he* did it—"

"Who? Mr. Partini? Who did what?"

"No, I couldn't see him—I couldn't see anyone, I just heard Marissa—"

"She's nuts," someone said and snickered, and Jinx leaned out the window.

"You shut up! And you—" He turned back to Ryan and stared.

"She said she wasn't here—but it was her voice— What's *wrong* with you?" Ryan broke off. "Why are you looking at me that way?"

"Just quit talking," Jinx said. "Here." He tossed her his jacket and hit the gas. "And don't bleed all over the seat—it's not my car."

As streets and intersections whizzed by, Ryan realized they were running lights and stop signs, and she looked over at Jinx's stony profile.

"You know you can't afford to get any more tickets," she scolded weakly. "You better slow down."

"Don't talk to me, McCauley."

"I couldn't stand it, Jinx, I just couldn't stand it anymore—I was so scared—"

"Okay, okay, I hear you—but—but did you have to do *this?"*

"I didn't realize—it was the only way out—I couldn't go back—"

"Just be quiet. Look—here's the hospital."

Ryan reached for her door, but Jinx already had it open, and he rushed her into the emergency room. In the bright, clean light, Ryan was surprised to see dark stains oozing through her towel, and as a nurse whisked her away, Jinx stood there, looking lost and confused.

"I'll call your mom, okay?"

Ryan could see him waving at her, but the pain was starting now, and she felt as if someone else's hands had gotten mixed up with hers. "No, don't call her! Don't leave me!"

"I'll be right here!"

What followed was a blur—white uniforms . . . questions . . . more pain—and through it all Ryan kept trying to *tell* them, to make them *listen,* but they just kept looking at her hands and then at each other with secretive looks, making her be quiet, making her sleep. . . .

"But you don't understand," she kept telling them. "It was the only way—nobody would help me—"

And the nods . . . the reassurances . . . the slipping away of time . . .

"Ryan? Honey, can you hear me? We can go home now."

Ryan stared at the pale green ceiling, and it seemed she'd been staring at it forever. She knew her thoughts had wandered, even though her eyes had been open all this time. She turned her head and saw Steve's and her mother's anxious faces.

"Why'd you do it?" Mrs. McCauley asked, her voice rising, but Steve put a hand on her shoulder, and she cut off with a guilty look.

"I had to get out," Ryan said. Her voice was thick, and she wanted to sleep. "I had to get out. That's all. It was the only way." *Why does everyone keep asking me that? I keep telling them, but they're not listening. . . .*

"It's my fault," Mrs. McCauley whispered, and she reached for Ryan's hand.

"No, it's not," Ryan mumbled. "I was just waiting like you said."

She saw her mother and Steve exchange blank looks.

"What's she talking about?" Mrs. McCauley whispered again, and again Steve patted her shoulder.

"Come on, Leslie, save it for another time."

Ryan stared at them, frowning. Strong arms helped her into a sitting position, and her head spun.

"How about a little ride?" Steve smiled.

"Only if I don't have to drive." Ryan got into the wheelchair, and Steve pushed her out into the lobby. To her surprise Jinx was still there—and with him Phoebe, Charles, and Winchester, who all stopped talking and stood up when they saw her. She stared at them in confusion. She suddenly felt angry, but wasn't sure why.

"Why are you all here?" she asked. *They're still doing it . . . everyone's still looking at me so funny. . . .*

"Oh, Ryan," Phoebe whispered, her eyes filling with tears. "Oh, I'm so sorry, I—"

"Phoebe, I'm fine, really, just a scratch." For the first time Ryan looked down and saw the bandages on her hands and wrists.

"Come on, Ryan," Mrs. McCauley said softly. "Let's just get you home."

And then, without warning, Ryan's anger turned to fear, and she grabbed Steve's hand and tried to stand up.

"But I don't need to go home! I'm fine! As a matter of fact, I'm hungry! Can't we all go out and get pizza or something? Jinx?" She looked wildly from face to face, each pair of eyes lowering in turn, refusing to meet her accusing stare. "Jinx?" she said again. "What's going on? What's wrong with everyone? What's—"

"You can see everyone later," Mrs. McCauley said, and Steve gently forced Ryan down again. "After you're better—after you've had a chance to—"

"Leslie," Steve interrupted. "Let's not talk about it now, okay? We agreed . . ."

Ryan tried to look back as Steve and her mother settled her into the car. "Where's Charles?"

"He had his car, and we came in mine," Mrs. McCauley said, trying to calm her.

"But why—why didn't he come with you?"

"He was supposed to pick you up. He was going to bring home hamburgers for dinner, and Steve asked if he'd mind getting you at work on the way."

"But *you* called. Why weren't *you* there?"

Her mother was looking at her as if she expected Ryan to attack her at any minute. "But I didn't call. I asked Charles to call. Ryan, what does it matter who came in which car or who called—"

"You weren't there. Charles wasn't there."

"Charles said he waited for you, but you never showed up. So he went to the shop and found the glass in the door broken. He was afraid there'd been a robbery, and he couldn't find you, so he called the police—"

"And in the meantime Jinx had called us," Steve picked up, "so we called the police, too, and the police called Mr. Partini—"

"Was the man in the store when Charles went in?" Ryan sat forward, her voice tight, pleading.

"Ryan, please, you've got to calm down—"

"The *man*, Mom—"

"What man? Ryan, what are you—"

"I need Charles," Ryan mumbled. She could see him standing outside the hospital talking to the others, and she lunged across her mother's lap to the window.

"Charles! Did you see the man! When you went into the toy shop, did you see the—"

"Ryan." Steve tried to pull her away. "Come on, kiddo, get back in the car—"

"No! Charles! Did you see him! Tell me you saw him!"

"Ryan, stop it!" Mrs. McCauley grabbed her and blocked the window. Steve hurriedly backed the car up and drove away.

"I need to ask him," Ryan whispered. "I need to talk to Charles . . . you don't understand . . ."

"Yes, yes, as soon as we get you home. Hush, now."

Ryan felt sick. She could see her mother and Steve exchanging looks over her head, and she choked on hot, burning tears.

"Almost there," Steve said cheerfully. "Almost home now, Ryan."

"A nice warm bed, won't that be nice?" Mrs. McCauley sounded peculiar, too cheerful, too strained. "I'll bring you some broth, you'll like that, won't you?"

"Why are you doing this?" Ryan murmured. "Why are you being so nice to me? I'm perfectly all right."

"Of course you are," her mother said quickly. "We know that, don't we, Steve? And you'll be even better once you see—"

"Leslie." Steve shook his head warningly, and Ryan stared at him. Something in the back of her mind sensed a change that she wasn't going to like, but she was too exhausted to care.

Mrs. McCauley and Steve got her upstairs into her mother's bed, and though Ryan kept protesting, nobody seemed to hear.

"You just take this medicine," Mrs. McCauley kept saying, "and when you wake up, we'll talk. When you feel better, we'll talk."

"I feel fine," Ryan insisted unhappily. "I want to sleep in my own room."

"You'll be fine in here," Mrs. McCauley said anxiously, smoothing Ryan's hair back from her forehead. It was something she hadn't done in a long, long time, and Ryan suddenly felt like crying. "And Charles is in your room, don't you remember?"

"Of course I remember. And where *is* Charles? I've got to ask him about the man. . . ." Ryan's eyelids drooped, and Steve and her mother shimmered, ghostly shadows. She tried to tell them, but they seemed to be growing dimmer, fading away from her. "Tried . . . to kill me," she mumbled.

"But we know you didn't mean it, Ryan. . . ." Her

mother's voice, down a long, dark tunnel. "We know you didn't, honey."

Mean what? Ryan's brain was all fuzzy, and she couldn't seem to concentrate. *Mean what—to get away from that horrible stranger—to break down the door so I wouldn't die in there?*

"Yes, I did," Ryan murmured. "Yes, I did mean to do it."

She thought she heard her mother crying, and then she slept—a fitful slumber of painful memories and haunted nightmares. Wild-eyed Santas chased her through streets that led nowhere, and every time she turned a corner, there stood Marissa, with blue skin and wide eyes, one arm pointing accusingly—*"I'm not here . . . I'm dead . . ."*

In the dream Ryan screamed and finally managed to wake herself up. She was drenched with sweat, and as she reached up to pull back her hair, she realized her hands wouldn't work, and she couldn't remember what had happened. Squinting into the dark, she tried to focus and saw a movement by the window.

"Marissa?" she murmured. "Marissa, what are you doing in my room?"

The figure barely stirred. Ryan thought it whispered to her, and she tried to sit up.

"Marissa . . . what is it? Why won't you talk to me?"

She leaned forward, her eyes widening, and the phantom moved again, coming nearer the bed.

"Don't scare me like that, Marissa, *don't scare me like that!*"

Ryan flung back the covers and blinked as the light came on, as her mother came into the room and pushed her gently back into bed.

"It's only a dream, honey, you're safe, don't be afraid—"

"Something moved there, Mom, by the window—"

"Curtains, that's all it is—ssh—"

"But my curtains don't look like that—"

"I know, honey, you're in my room, remember?"

And she did remember then, about everything that had happened, and she fell back upon the pillows with a groan.

"My hands hurt, Mom."

"I know, but they'll be better soon. Here—take this medicine. Try to sleep now."

"No—Marissa's here, Mom, in the room with me—"

"You only dreamed it, Ryan. Marissa's not here."

"No . . . I remember . . . Marissa's dead. I killed her."

"Oh, Ryan . . ."

The darkness hid Mrs. McCauley's face, but Ryan could tell her mother was crying. She heard the door click shut and then a lowered exchange of voices just outside in the hall.

"I really don't think I should leave you like this," Steve's voice, serious and concerned. "The doctor said she's just about over the edge as it is."

"Of course you have to leave. It's so important for you—"

"Not as important as you and Ryan. Come on,

Leslie, there'll be other chances. Suppose something happens and you need me—"

"No." Mrs. McCauley's voice, firm and stubborn. "You've been praying for this opportunity, Steve—we both have. It may not come again. I *want* you to go. I know Ryan would, too."

"I'm not leaving. It's a terrible time to even think—"

"If you don't, I'll never speak to you again. I mean it. Look, Charles is here if I need anything. And I have lots of friends to help. For goodness' sake, you'll only be gone a few days—how much can happen in a day or two?"

"It looks to me like a hell of a lot has happened already." There was a guilty pause, and Steve's voice grew quieter. "Then at least let me change my flight. Let me wait till tomorrow."

"Absolutely not. You know we can't depend on the fog in the morning—and you need to get there on time!"

"I'm only thinking of Ryan . . . of what she's been through—"

"And I'm thinking of Ryan, too," her mother said sadly. "How's she going to feel when this gets out?"

Ryan frowned, straining her ears to hear. *What's she talking about?*

Steve sighed. "There must be something we can do."

"Nothing we can say is going to stop all the gossip. Especially this kind." Her mother sounded hurt. "There she is, lying in there confused and in pain, and

I'm not helping her. I've only been thinking of myself!"

"Come on, Leslie . . . you've both been through a hell of a lot."

"Yes, but I've had you to lean on through all this, and she's been alone. I just didn't realize she was so fragile!" Mom's voice broke, and she began to cry again. "And by tomorrow it'll be all over town . . . everyone will know that Ryan tried to kill herself."

Chapter 18

*K*ill myself!

Ryan's brain reeled, and she grabbed the edge of the bed.

Kill myself! What's she talking about . . . ?

As Steve's and her mother's voices faded out of earshot, Ryan held her hands in front of her face, her eyes piercing the darkness. She could feel the pain now, dull and throbbing, *and so it must be real, I haven't imagined the pain, so I must not be crazy, they just don't know, they couldn't know because they weren't there. . . .*

Trying not to make any noise, Ryan fumbled with the phone on the nightstand and torturously dialed Phoebe's number. The phone rang and rang, and just as she was about to give up, Ryan heard Mrs. Evans's cheery hello.

"Mrs. Evans"—her voice shook—"Mrs. Evans . . . this is Ryan."

Something was wrong. She could tell immediately from the long uncomfortable silence, and then the careful calmness of Mrs. Evans's voice when she finally spoke again.

"Yes, Ryan. How are you feeling, dear? We heard you had . . . an accident."

She knows. . . . Ryan closed her eyes and fought back tears. *She thinks she knows what's happened, but she's wrong*—"May I speak to Phoebe, please?"

"Phoebe?" There was an awkward pause. Ryan had the distinct feeling that Mrs. Evans had covered the mouthpiece and was whispering to someone. When she spoke again, she sounded strained. "Well . . . Ryan . . . this really isn't a . . . a good time right now. Could Phoebe—"

"Why won't she talk to me, Mrs. Evans?" Ryan demanded. She was trying not to raise her voice, trying not to cry, and she *knew* Phoebe was there, she *knew* it—"Why won't she come to the phone? It's not what you think—why won't you believe—"

Surprised, she heard the dial tone and looked down to see her own hand on the telephone. *I hung it up myself. Who needs Phoebe, anyway? I don't need anyone*—

Sick at heart, Ryan crawled back under the covers, and tried to sleep. She could hear the clock ticking . . . minutes dragging by into endless hours. She heard Steve and Mom saying their goodbyes in the down-stairs hall, then a little while later, her mother's heartbroken sobs from the living room. She wouldn't cry for long, Ryan knew—it would only take a couple of the usual sleeping pills, and her mother would be oblivious till morning. Ryan wondered where Charles was, and what he'd been doing all evening—she hadn't heard him in the house, but maybe he'd been

making himself inconspicuous throughout all this tragedy she'd seemed to cause. *My fault again . . . everything's always my fault . . .*

It started to snow. She could see it from the bed, laciness drifting past the window. She dozed . . . woke . . . dozed again. The night waned, and she never knew when the snow let up, and she never knew what woke her, bringing her up from terrible dreams, tapping softly against her window. . . .

Ryan opened her eyes. She saw the pewter sky of early morning and, upon the windowpane, dribbles of clinging snow. Lying there, she tried to slip back into her twilight state, but as she gazed through half-open lids at the window, something hit the glass and came apart in soft flurries.

A snowball?

Puzzled, Ryan tried to raise herself on her elbows. Almost at once the pain stabbed through her hands and wrists, and she bit her lip to keep from crying out. She didn't want to remember yesterday or what she'd have to face today—

Splat! The windowpane rattled as more white softness exploded against the glass. Ryan frowned and pushed back the covers. It *was* a snowball—but who would be out throwing snowballs at this hour?

The world was bathed in shadowy light as she pressed her face to the glass and peered down into the backyard. Fresh wet snow clung everywhere, giving the lawn a surreal appearance that Ryan found unsettling. Her breath fogged up the glass, and she winced as she tried to rub clumsily at the pane . . .

And then she saw it.

There on the lawn, just beneath her window, a huge, three-tiered snowman, at least six feet tall.

As Ryan gazed in wonder, she saw its long stick arms, reaching toward the sky . . . the ends branched out, like fingers, desperately clawing . . .

She saw the round oversize head . . .

She saw the face—not on the *front* of the head looking outward, but rather on *top* of the head, so that it looked straight up at her window.

From where Ryan stood, the eyes were empty black holes.

The mouth formed a silent scream.

And fluttering around its head in the morning breeze were long, red ribbons.

Chapter 19

NO!"

Ryan raced to the kitchen and out the back door, her screams exploding with unbearable fury. She didn't even feel the cold as she raced into the yard and attacked the snowman, tearing it apart. She didn't hear the running footsteps on the porch behind her, didn't even know anyone was there until she fell down, exhausted, and saw her mother and Charles huddled together on the steps. In the gray morning Mrs. McCauley's voice carried across the lawn, and it sounded terrified.

"Ryan . . . my God . . . what are you—"

"Make it stop!" Ryan screamed, and she pointed to the snow heaped around her. "Please, Mom— *please!*"

"Oh . . . oh, Ryan . . ."

"This isn't the first time!" Ryan shouted, and she tried to stand, but her legs wouldn't hold her. "I've seen Marissa before—"

Mrs. McCauley looked frantically at Charles, who started forward slowly, as if afraid of making a wrong move.

"I know I'm not crazy!" Ryan babbled. "I tried to hold her—I wouldn't have left her there! If I'd known she was serious, I wouldn't have gone off—"

"What's she talking about, Charles? Oh, Ryan, come here to me—"

"I wish it'd been me!" And suddenly Ryan was laughing uncontrollably, digging through the snow, holding up lumps of charcoal and long strings of curly Christmas ribbon. "I don't know what's happening! I'm so sick of all this, I just wish I were *dead!*"

Mrs. McCauley covered her face with her hands, and Charles moved past her, reaching Ryan in four long strides, trying to coax her gently to her feet. Ryan pushed him and sent him sprawling.

"We have to tell her! No, don't tell her—get away from me! I wish you'd never come!"

"I'm calling the doctor." Mrs. McCauley headed into the house, but not before Ryan had time to fling a final comment.

"Yes! Call him! I'm not the sick one here—I'm the *alive* one! Remember me? I'm the one you'd rather have dead, only I'm still here!"

Charles managed to grab her at last, and as Ryan kicked and fought him, he dragged her back into the house. At the foot of the staircase he lifted her into his arms and started up.

"Put her in my room, Charles." Mrs. McCauley was following them, wringing her hands, and after another brief struggle, Ryan went limp. She didn't resist as Charles lowered her into bed; she lay there calmly and closed her eyes to shut out their stares.

"Ryan—"

Mrs. McCauley's hand lingered on her forehead, but Ryan jerked her head away. She wished they would go away and leave her alone. She felt like that snowman down there—crushed and crumpled and flat.

"Ryan"—her mother sat down on the bed, talking fast—"it's going to be okay, honey—you're going to start seeing a very nice doctor."

"You're sending me to a psychiatrist. And then you're locking me up."

"Locking you up! Of course we're not locking you up! Where would you ever get such an idea?"

"Please lock me up." Without warning Ryan sat up and grabbed her mother's shoulders, her eyes pleading. "Please lock me up, Mom, I want you to. Then maybe all these scary things will stop happening to me—"

"Ryan, no one is going to lock you up—"

"Just leave me alone, then." She saw Charles framed in the doorway, and she hated the look on his face, so sad, so sorry—"Just go away."

The phone rang, but Mrs. McCauley ignored the one on her nightstand. Nodding to Charles, she went out into the hallway, and he followed, closing the door behind them. Ryan could barely hear her mother talking in the kitchen, and then someone turned the radio on, and she couldn't hear anymore. She lay there and watched the sky change from gray to pearl, more snow clouds piling up, quilting the sky, and the bedside clock ticking toward schooltime. Ryan had no intention of going to school today—or any day from now on. She knew she'd never be able to face anyone there—the stares and whispers, the phony, sympathetic smiles . . .

Someone's after me, and I'm all alone. Charles knows, but he can't stop what's happening.

Mrs. McCauley didn't want to go to work—Ryan could hear Charles offering to drive her, promising to come right back. Ryan was glad when they'd gone, yet she was also terrified to be alone in the house. She groped her way carefully downstairs and checked all the doors. She made herself some hot tea, then sat down at the table to think. *For a while I was the only one who thought I was going crazy . . . but now everyone else thinks so, too, so I really must be. . . .*

The tea warmed her a little. She could feel her nerves relaxing and her mind began to calm and clear. She thought about last night—her terror in the toyshop—the patronizing way everyone had looked at her at the hospital. . . . She knew she had to stop going over it before she started crying again. She went upstairs to Marissa's room and stood in the doorway and stared.

The aching in her heart was almost more than she could stand, and she pictured Marissa on the window seat, the way she'd be staring back with a smug smile.

It's normal for everyone to miss you so much . . . you were the pretty one, the popular one . . . you were everything Mom always wanted in a daughter—

The room seemed to hurt around her, the silence long and grieving.

"But still," Ryan whispered, "still . . . I know we fought . . . I know sometimes we even hated each other—but—I never would have left if I thought you were in danger." Tears burned her throat, and she could hardly speak. "You know that, don't you . . . you know I wouldn't have let anything happen to you. And now . . . I could be next . . ."

As Ryan gazed at the windowpane, the sun struggled free of the clouds, and in that instant a ray of light shimmered on the glass, slanting down across one photograph on the crowded sill.

Marissa.

She was sitting in a chair, going through a pile of things in her lap, and someone had obviously surprised her into looking up. She was smiling straight at Ryan, and in the picture she was holding a bunch of photographs.

Photographs . . .

As Ryan stared at the golden shaft of light, it vanished.

She walked over to Marissa's desk and rummaged through the phone book. She picked up the phone and called the number of the drugstore.

"Good morning, may I help you?"

She took a deep breath and leaned against the desk. "I'd like to see if my pictures are ready, please."

"Sure. Your name?"

"McCauley. Ryan."

"Just a minute."

Ryan could hear voices laughing. Drawers opened and papers rustled. Someone picked up the receiver again.

"McCauley, you said?"

"Yes."

"Sorry. There's nothing here."

Ryan stared, seeing nothing. Pain crept slowly up her arms.

"But there has to be. They said I could pick them up today."

"When did you bring them in?"

"Saturday. Late afternoon."

"Hmmm . . . okay. Hang on a minute."

More rummaging, then finally the voice back again, apologetic.

"One of the girls says someone picked them up earlier."

"Are you sure?" Ryan asked. "Who was it? Who picked them up?"

"She says it was a guy," the voice said. "She was at the counter, but she didn't wait on him."

"What'd he look like?"

The voice mumbled, then came back. "She wasn't really paying attention, but she heard him give his name—Ryan McCauley."

"No, I'm—" Ryan broke off, shaking her head impatiently. "Never mind. Thanks."

She walked slowly to the window, staring out at the wintry day, a feeling of dread washing over her.

Charles must have gone by and picked them up, and as soon as he brings them home, then we'll know for sure, we'll finally know the truth one way or the other—

The telephone shrilled into the silence. Heart pounding, Ryan picked it up.

"Hello?"

"Mrs. McCauley?"

"No, she's not here right now. Can I take a message?"

"Well . . ." The voice sounded businesslike, but now it hesitated. "This is Officer John Henley from the sheriff's department. I need to speak to Mrs. McCauley—it's in regard to the death of Marissa McCauley."

Ryan went icy all over. "Yes! This is Ryan! I'm Mrs. McCauley's daughter! What is it?"

"Well, ma'am . . ." Another long pause, then a burst of static. Ryan clutched the receiver, wincing.

"Are you there? What *is* it? Are you there?"

The voice came back, even more solemn than before. "The truth is, ma'am, we've located a body over near Platt Valley. A farmer discovered it about an hour ago, and we think it might be—"

"Oh, God, oh, God, where is she? Where are you?"

"—could come down here to make a positive identification—"

"Yes! Yes! Where are you again?" Ryan was trying to get through the door, the cord stretching as far as it could.

"Platt Valley," the voice said again. "Are you familiar with—"

"I think so, yes! I think I know where it is—"

"Ten Mile Road . . . you take the northeast turnoff, about twenty miles to a farm—"

"Yes, I'll find it, I'm coming right now. Wait for me—will you wait for me?"

"Yes, ma'am," the voice said soberly. "We'll be right here."

Ryan hurtled down the stairs and through the kitchen, grabbing up her jacket and purse as she ran. Mom's car was in the garage, but the keys that were usually in the ignition weren't there.

"Damn!" Racing back to the kitchen, Ryan pulled open a drawer so fast that it flew off its rollers, spilling all its contents onto the floor. She fell to her knees, digging through all the junk until she found an extra set of keys. She was halfway out the door when the phone rang again.

She wasn't going to answer it, but as Ryan hesitated the thought suddenly came to her that it might be her mother. Making a split-second decision, she raced back and snatched up the receiver.

"Hello?"

"It wasn't my idea to call—Mom wants to know if—"

"Jinx—I can't talk—I have to go—oh, Jinx—"

"Oh, McCauley."

"They found Marissa—I mean, I think they found Marissa—"

"What? Wait a minute, where?"

"I have to go! Down at Platt Valley out on Ten Mile Road—I have to go identify her—"

"Ryan, wait a minute—is your mom there?"

"No, it's just me, I have to go!"

She took off at a run, dropping the receiver, leaving the phone cord banging against the wall.

She didn't hear Jinx calling after her.

She didn't hear the concern in his voice or the way it suddenly turned to fear.

"But they wouldn't have you identify it there, would they?" he shouted. "Wouldn't you go to the morgue?"

Chapter 20

Out on the road Ryan racked her brain, trying to remember exactly where her turnoff was. The sky seemed to press down on all sides, and she grimaced as the first spatter of snow and ice slid down the windshield.

She urged the car to go faster, hanging on painfully to the steering wheel. Within minutes what had started as a flurry became a slushy downpour. Ryan turned on the wipers and hunched forward, squinting. She could already feel slick spots beneath the tires. *This is unbelievable . . . I can hardly see the road. . . .*

She flipped on the radio and groaned as she heard the winter storm warning. *I can't have a wreck . . . I have to get to Marissa. . . .* She tried to find a familiar landmark, but the snowy fields were changing shape before her eyes. Nervously watching ice build up on her wiper blades, she passed the turnoff before she realized and tried to brake on the icy blacktop. Heart pounding, she slammed into reverse and whipped onto the side road.

I wonder what she'll look like. . . . Horrified, Ryan tried to stop her mind from its imaginings, but she couldn't seem to turn it off. *Will her skin be blue—stop it stop it stop it!* Tears blurred her eyes, and as she blinked them away, she missed a curve and slid toward a tree. She turned into the skid and managed to straighten the car in time. The wind was blowing so hard, it was like driving into a swirling tunnel.

Ryan tasted blood and realized she'd bitten her lip. The wipers were barely moving now, they were so encrusted with ice. How much farther? Ten miles? Fifteen? She had no idea how far she'd come. She rubbed hard at the windshield, trying to clear away the fog. As the wheels gave a sudden jerk, the car plowed into a snowbank.

Ryan floored the gas pedal, but the wheels spun helplessly on ice. Fighting off a wave of panic, she shut off the engine and opened her door.

Miraculously she thought she saw a rooftop in the distance, and she started toward it. As the roof materialized into a building, Ryan called out and saw a vague human form suddenly appear through the snow. For just a moment it seemed to be listening, but then it disappeared.

Ryan could see the barn clearly now, not ten yards ahead. As she called again, she noticed the open doorway, and the human figure framed there, as though it were waiting for her.

"Hello! I'm stuck in the snow! I'm trying to find—"

The words caught in her throat. As she looked up in horror, she saw the lumpy coat . . . the black ski mask . . . the eyeholes staring back—

"No!" Ryan tried to run, but she was no match for

his uncanny speed. Dragging her into the barn, he chuckled softly and barred the doors behind her.

At first she couldn't see a thing. The darkness yawned emptily around her, smelling of damp wood and straw. As Ryan picked herself up from the floor, a dim light began to focus in one far corner, and a lantern threw ghostly shadows up the drafty walls.

"Oh, God, who are you? Where's the police?"

Helplessly she felt her arms twisted behind her as he forced her to the back of the barn. She didn't even have time to brace herself for the fall—as the yawning hole appeared without warning in the floor, she hurtled through it and landed on a cushion of cold, prickly straw. Dazed, she scooted back into a corner and blinked against the gloom. She could see the ski mask, floating in the hole above her head, and as she felt a movement near her feet, she realized she wasn't alone. Terrified, she watched as a human shadow pulled itself from the darkness and began to glide toward her, a flickering lantern held high above its head.

"Ryan McCauley"—the voice sounded amused, echoing through the blackness, sending chills up her spine—"so glad you could join us."

"Who—who are you? Where's Marissa?" Her voice shook uncontrollably, filling the space with her fear.

"Marissa?" The shadow moved closer, pulsing up the damp stone walls. "Well . . . of course she's not here . . . but I'll take you to her."

"The police," Ryan murmured. "Where are they? They called and—" She froze as the approaching figure stepped out at last into a sickly pool of yellow light. "Oh, my God . . . Charles . . ."

"You do want to see her, don't you?" he asked smoothly, a faint smile creeping over his face. "Just to be together again . . ."

"What are you doing here? How did you know about Marissa? How—" She broke off as her eyes probed her shadowy surroundings . . . as they swept over the piles and piles of clear plastic bags . . . the snowy drifts of powder inside . . . "What—"

"Come on, now, Ryan, surely you've watched enough TV to recognize drugs when you see them." Charles laughed softly. "Marissa recognized them. She even took pictures of . . . shall we say . . . a business transaction?" He set the lantern down carefully on the floor, but his smile never wavered. "Thank goodness I picked up that film in time. Thank goodness I believed her when she said she'd uncovered a scandal. Otherwise . . . a lot of people would have been in a whole lot of trouble."

Ryan's mouth fell open. *"You!* You were selling drugs on campus and Marissa found out! You're the one she took pictures of—it was you all—"

"No, no, no." Another chuckle, as if the whole matter were unbearably comical. "I'm too smart to be photographed, Ryan. It's just too bad everyone isn't as smart as me."

"Then . . . who . . ."

"It was a perfect little setup, you have to admit." Charles crossed his arms and leaned back against the wall. "Basing the whole operation right here in this boring little town—who would have thought it would be so easy? We couldn't let Marissa ruin it, now, could we? Not with all the millions at stake. It was only fair . . . she tried to stop us . . . so naturally . . . we had to stop *her.*"

"You killed her!" Ryan screamed. "You killed my sister!"

Charles's face registered exaggerated distaste. "Ryan, I'm surprised at you! I have more class than to dirty my hands with something so unpleasant—especially when there are other people around who are so good at it!"

She saw him staring into the space above their heads . . . she saw his smile widening . . . and as she looked up, she saw the lumpy coat fall away . . . the ski mask peeling back from the shadowed face. And suddenly she was back again, back at the river that horrible day, trying to rescue Marissa, Marissa's terrified screams echoing over and over in her head—*"sleeve—sleeve"*—and Ryan had tried so hard to hang on, had tried so hard to keep hold of Marissa's sleeve . . .

Only she hadn't been saying *sleeve.*

Swallowing water, fighting for her life, Marissa hadn't been saying *sleeve* at all . . .

And now, as the black ski mask fell through the air and landed at her feet, Ryan saw Steve grinning down at her.

Chapter 21

No . . ." Ryan murmured, "no . . . I don't believe this . . ."

As the shadows swayed around her, she strained against the wall and fought for air. Sobs caught in her throat, and she choked them back down again as she saw Charles and Steve exchange satisfied glances.

"Do you think I could have had a life," Steve said reasonably, "wondering just how much Marissa knew? I thought I saw her that day with her camera, but I couldn't be sure . . . not till she told Charles she had evidence of something that was so important. We were talking about my whole future . . . my reputation . . . all my new prospects . . . even my bank accounts. I couldn't let her destroy what I'd worked so hard for. There was too much tied up in everything . . . way too much at stake."

As Ryan stared at him numbly, he shook his head and shrugged.

"But it wasn't just me. She would have ruined a lot of people's lives. So you have to weigh the consequences . . . one life for all that money. All that freedom. There's really no decision when you look at it that way, is there? We did the only thing we could do."

Charles shook a finger condescendingly. "And then Marissa got you into it, Ryan. How were we supposed to know how much she'd told you? Steve went through as many of her things as he could after she died . . . as many of *your* things as he could when no one was in the house . . . but how could we really know what you knew? Maybe there were things you repressed about Marissa's accident . . . maybe you would have remembered them later on. . . . How could we live under that shadow, always waiting for you to remember? You wouldn't talk to anyone about it. You wouldn't confide in anyone. So I decided to come for a little visit. But you didn't trust me, either, did you? Not until you got really scared. . . ."

"And you were so easy to scare." Steve sighed. "It takes time to drive someone right out of her mind . . . to make it believable. You felt so guilty about Marissa, it was almost too easy. A few unfortunate accidents . . . a tape from Marissa's answering machine at school . . . some great disguises . . . and then that necklace I grabbed at the last minute . . . an afterthought, really. The game's not nearly so much fun when there's no challenge. And you were so good at helping us, too . . . everyone thinks you tried to do yourself in. Charles and your mother *heard* you say you wanted to die. . . ." He bit his lip and tried to hold back a smile. "So no one will really be surprised when you kill yourself . . . for real this time."

"It was the film." Charles patted his coat pocket.

"These photos. We couldn't really be sure Marissa had proof until you remembered the film. And now, of course, we can't afford to keep you around."

Ryan made a desperate move toward the ladder, but Charles caught her and pushed her back down.

"Uh-uh, now, Ryan, don't be a bad girl. You wanted for it all to be over, didn't you? So we're really doing you a favor. We're helping you be with Marissa again."

"You can't do this," Ryan choked. "Think about Mom—"

"But I am thinking of her." Steve looked perfectly at ease. "I'm thinking what a wonderful life we'll have with all that money . . . her being so destroyed by the untimely deaths of her two daughters, that she'll be the perfect little wife . . . always do what I say . . . always depend on me and please me so I don't leave her. She's my perfect cover. I should really thank you, Ryan. Sacrificing yourself for our happiness. But then, you always were such a good girl." He stretched languorously and flexed his fingers. "Well, I better get to work. There can't be a suicide till we cut through that ice." He started to say something more when there was a series of thuds behind him, as if someone were pounding on the barn door. As Steve disappeared from view, Ryan lunged at Charles. The struggle lasted only a minute—as she fell back once more into the corner, Charles pointed his gun at her and cocked the hammer.

"Come on, Ryan, don't be stupid. It'll be so much

more romantic to fling yourself into the river than to shoot yourself in the head. . . ."

"Please let me go," she begged. "I won't say anything, I swear! You'll never have to worry—we can pretend none of this ever hap—" She broke off at the sudden disturbance of voices overhead. It sounded as though there was an argument going on, and as the voices came nearer, she cringed back into the shadows and tried not to look at Charles's pistol.

"Where is she?" a stern voice demanded, and as Ryan gazed up fearfully, another face hung there, disembodied, in the empty blackness, caught in a feeble web of lantern light.

Ryan's heart turned to ice. She felt tears on her cheeks, and a cry lodged in her throat.

"Ah, *Bambalina*," Mr. Partini said gently, "why couldn't you mind your own business, eh?"

"Oh, my God—Mr.—oh, my God—"

"I never want to hurt you"—he spread his hands helplessly—"but there's no other way! Ah, why you hurt me so much, Ryan—another bad, bad heartache!"

Over the toymaker's shoulder Steve looked anxious. "We better get to work—we have appointments—"

"I try to keep you out of it," Mr. Partini said sadly. "The toys . . . you want to deliver . . . I always say no. You never find out they hide the cocaine . . . you and me, we stay good friends. Who would ever think this sister of yours would be snooping around? That she could cause so much trouble for all of us?" He shook his head—"No, *Bambalina* . . ."—I never think this will happen, eh?"

"Mr. Partini, *please!* You've *got* to help me! You've got to *do* some—"

"Take care of her." He nodded to Steve, then motioned to Charles with one frail hand. "I no like my friends to suffer."

He and Steve both twisted around as a flurry of snow and ice swept through the barn . . . as raised voices shouted from the front.

"Now what?" Mr. Partini snapped, and as Charles started up the ladder, the old man looked down with an amused smile. "How nice to have so many visitors today!"

Before Ryan could even scream, a body plummeted down through the trapdoor and lay motionless in the straw.

Chapter 22

Jinx! Oh, Jinx—what have you *done* to him!"

Ryan knelt beside the still figure . . . saw blood smeared over the dirty straw. "You'll never get away with this! I'll make *all* of you pay—I swear—"

"Ah, poor Ryan." Mr. Partini shook his head. "Why didn't you just kill the boy outside, eh, if it make her so upset—"

"What! Did you say Ryan!" And as Mr. Partini was pushed roughly aside, Winchester peered down, stricken. "Ryan—my God—what are you—"

"I hate you!" Ryan screamed. "How could you do this! How—"

"What is she doing here?" Winchester demanded. He was staring at Charles, and even in the dim light his face was unnaturally pale. "What are you doing to her? Why is she down here—"

"There, there, delivery boy, calm down." Mr. Partini chuckled softly. "You got lots to do— customers are waiting, eh?"

"You can't do anything to her—" Winchester turned to the old man, his voice bewildered. "She doesn't know anything about anything—she told me so—"

"Yes, yes, and of course you believed her." Mr. Partini nodded patiently, waving one hand. "But now we know different, eh? And so . . ."

"You can't," Winchester whispered. "You never said anything about this . . . you promised no one would get hurt. . . ."

"But Marissa got hurt." Charles gave a derisive laugh. "How did you think that happened so conveniently?"

"She fell." Winchester's voice was numb. "She had an accident and fell . . . through . . . the . . ." As his voice trailed away, he shook his head slowly. "No. No . . . I don't believe you. . . ."

"Is a matter of survival." Mr. Partini shrugged. "Survival of the fittest. When you became one of us, I thought you understood—"

"I made those deliveries for you because I didn't know what they were at first," Winchester said flatly. "I only thought they were toys—"

"But you stayed. And your loyalty is touching." The old man put a hand to his heart. "Don't you agree, boys."

"Loyalty had nothing to do with it. You threatened to hurt my family. To burn down my father's business. I didn't have a choice."

"And you don't have one now, as far as I can see." Charles raised his eyebrows and met Steve's expression with a smug smile. "Your job is to take orders. So take them."

Winchester was staring from one to the other, as if he couldn't believe what was happening. "Look . . . I've done everything you wanted . . . but you can't hurt her, do you understand? You can't—"

"Poor little brothers and sisters . . ." Mr. Partini shook his head solemnly, wiping invisible tears from his eyes. "Poor little ones . . . such nasty accidents that kids can fall into—"

Charles climbed up and handed the gun to Winchester. "We'll be back in a few minutes, so keep them nice and quiet. Oh . . . and Winchester . . . don't screw up."

The voices faded eerily into the black cavern of the barn. There was a shriek of wind . . . and then . . . deathly quiet.

Ryan gazed up at Winchester through a blur of tears. She could feel Jinx rousing, trying to lift his head. As he moaned and turned over, she looked down and wiped the stream of blood from his nose.

"Jinx—are you all right?" It seemed such a hopeless thing to say as she put one hand to his cheek. "Did you break anything?"

"Dammit, McCauley," Jinx mumbled, pressing a fist to his gushing nose, "what the hell have you gotten us into this time?"

"They're going to kill me," Ryan said, surprised at how calm and resigned she sounded. "They're going to throw me in the river and make it look like suicide—they're going—"

She jumped back with a scream as Winchester

landed lightly beside them. He started to lean over Jinx, but Ryan shoved him away.

"No! Don't you touch him! You leave him alone!"

"There's a back way," Winchester said quietly, motioning them to hold their voices down. "Mr. Partini's gone, and Charles and Steve are on the other side of the barn, so they won't see you. Here're my keys. I want you to take my truck and—"

"Your truck?" Jinx murmured. "That old thing'll never make it—"

"Use the radio to call the police. Don't hang around, understand? Just get out of here!"

"But—but what about you?" Jinx had sat up now and was trying to get his bearings. "We can't just leave you—when they find out you let us go—"

"No." Winchester gave a faint smile, shaking his head. "They're going to kill me anyway. Now, hurry —we can't waste any more time."

"It was all planned, wasn't it?" Ryan peered miserably into his face, "that night when Charles let me out of the van. He really was trying to kill me—"

"I was supposed to find you—to get you to trust me—so maybe you'd talk and tell me what you knew. Steve and Charles had both tried to get you to open up to them, and they thought you might confide in me. . . ." Winchester's face darkened. "I never wanted to hurt you, Ryan. You have to believe that. And I didn't lie about wanting you to stay that night. I've liked you for a long time. The only reason I ever went out with Marissa in the first place was to try to meet you."

Ryan swallowed a lump in her throat. She looked at Jinx in panic. "We can't just leave him—"

"It'll be safer for you if I can distract them. Go on." Winchester grabbed her elbow and jerked her to her feet. "They'll be back any second—hurry—"

They got up the ladder and raced to the other end of the barn. As Winchester held the lantern high, Ryan spotted a door camouflaged in the rear wall of one of the stalls, and she reached nervously for Jinx while Winchester struggled with the rusted latch. Without warning the door blew open on a blast of icy wind.

"This way!" Winchester herded them through. "Keep running—whatever you do, don't stop! Don't come back!"

As Ryan saw the door closing, she was seized with a sudden premonition of tragedy. "No!" She tried to wedge herself in the doorway. "Come with us! You've got to come with us—"

She felt Jinx pulling her, saw the quick flash of tenderness in Winchester's eyes as he thrust her away from the door.

"Take care of her, Jinx!" he said. "Now, run!"

Ryan couldn't even see where they were going. The wind tore at them from all sides, pelting them ruthlessly with ice and snow. As she slipped and stumbled, Jinx forced her to her feet and dragged her on.

"I think I see the truck!"

"Where?"

"We're almost there—come on, Ryan—just a little more—"

As tow truck suddenly appeared through the

white, swirling eddies, Ryan flung open the door and fell inside.

"We're going to make it!" she said breathlessly. "Oh, hurry, Jinx—hurry!"

Beside her Jinx fumbled the key into the ignition and gave it a turn. Nothing happened. Casting a wild look at Ryan, he slammed his fist against the dashboard and turned the key again. The engine ground slowly several times, then stopped.

"Damn!" Jinx pumped the accelerator . . . jiggled the key. "Try the radio!"

Ryan looked at him helplessly. "I don't know how to work it!"

She saw him start to lean toward the dashboard—she saw his door suddenly burst open—but before she could scream, Charles had Jinx around the neck, bending him backward out the door.

"Bad idea," he sneered at them. "Tricks like that make me very . . . very angry—"

"Get out of there!" Outside Ryan's window Steve pounded the roof with his gun and put his other hand on the door. "I'm going to enjoy this, Ryan"—he pushed his face to the glass, his features grotesquely distorted—"even more than I enjoyed killing Marissa —even more than—"

"Shut up! Look at the barn!" As Charles broke in excitedly, his grip loosened around Jinx's neck, and Steve straightened with a look of alarm.

"What's wrong?"

"The damn thing's on fire!"

Jinx moved so quickly that Ryan scarcely realized what happened. Twisting out of Charles's grasp, Jinx shoved him backward into the snow and slammed the door, flooring the gas pedal as he thrust the key in one last time. With a hoarse groan the engine sputtered, tried to die, then turned over at last—and the truck lurched into action, fishtailing through the snow as Jinx tried desperately to find the road.

Something ricocheted against the roof. As the truck shook violently, Jinx glanced in the rearview mirror and reached out for Ryan.

"Get down! They're shooting at us!"

As another bullet struck, he swerved, flinging Ryan hard into her door. She tried to sit back up again, but the truck spun wildly, and she hit the dashboard before she could catch herself.

"Get down!" Jinx yelled again. "Get down on the—"

His words were drowned out by the crash of breaking glass. Ryan screamed as she saw the back window come apart—as she felt sharp slivers spray across the side of her head and her shoulders. Jinx was shouting to her, trying to steer the truck, trying to push her down onto the seat.

"Are you okay?"

"I don't know—I think I might have gotten hit—"

The truck slowed down . . . slid the last few feet to a stop. As Jinx grabbed her, she shook uncontrollably and pulled her hand away from her head, staring down in amazement at the fresh smear of blood.

"You're okay, Ryan, you hear me? It's just the glass—you're not shot—you're just cut—"

Ryan shrieked in terror. As Jinx swung around, Charles's gun exploded through the window in a hail of flying glass. Jinx slammed back against the seat, and as Ryan screamed again, Charles thrust his gun against Jinx's face and tightened on the trigger.

"Merry Christmas, Ryan," he snarled.

The gun exploded, a deafening roar that went on and on, spattering the seat, the dash, the windows with blood. As Ryan stared in paralyzed horror, Charles's body twisted crazily, then went limp, hanging half inside the truck like a disfigured doll. She saw his head lift slowly as he stared at her with wild, glazed eyes, and then suddenly his whole body jerked, falling away as the door burst open.

"Get out of here!" Winchester shouted, hanging on to the door. "Steve's right behind me! *Go!*"

To Ryan's dismay, the truck roared back into action. She could see Jinx sagging over the steering wheel, blood gushing down his face, and Winchester against the side of the truck, yelling directions as he tried to dodge bullets and balance on the running board.

It seemed they drove through the snow forever.

From some remote corner of her mind, Ryan realized they were slowing down at last . . . stopping in an unfamiliar place where everything was quiet and hidden. She saw Winchester's haggard face beside her . . . she heard the pain in Jinx's voice as he kept his head turned away.

"I'll take you," Jinx whispered. "Wherever you say . . . wherever you want to go . . ."

The silence went on and on.

"To town, then," Winchester said softly. "To the police."

Ryan closed her eyes and cried.

Chapter 23

He's turning state's witness," Jinx said. "He'll testi-
fy against Steve and Mr. Partini . . . the police promised it'd go easier on him, and he wants to do it."

Ryan looked up from the bench in the hallway,
trying to ignore the uniformed officers hurrying by.

"Then . . . Charles is . . ."

"He was already dead when the police got there,"
Jinx said, his voice lowering. "Winchester saw the
whole thing—Steve trying to shoot him *and* us. He's
going to tell them all about the toyshop and the
deliveries, too. All the evidence probably burned up
when he set fire to the barn, but he's pretty sure where
all the other drugs are hidden. He knows about some
of the things they did to scare you. And with you and
me to tell how Winchester saved our lives . . ."

Ryan's voice shook. "But it wasn't his fault. They
threatened his family. . . . Did you say how they
threatened to hurt his family and how he was just
trying to protect the people he loves?"

Jinx stared at her as she bent her head and tried to
regain her composure. "I guess they're finally through

talking to me—how about you?" At her nod he added, "I told my mom she didn't have to hang around. The snow's stopped now, and I kinda feel like walking home. How's *your* mom?"

"Still in there talking to the police." Ryan sighed. As she pressed a soggy tissue to her lashes, she felt Jinx awkwardly touch her shoulder. "Oh, God, Jinx, my poor mom . . . first Marissa and now Steve. I can't imagine how she must feel."

"Pretty lucky," Jinx said. "'Cause she's got you."

Ryan looked up at him, her eyes brimming. "Some luck. Everyone thinks I'm crazy. Everyone thinks I tried to kill myself. I'll never be able to show my face at school again. I don't even have a best friend anymore—the last time I tried to call Phoebe, she wouldn't even talk to me."

Jinx shook his head. "Not true. She was really upset about you going to the hospital—she was crying so hard, Mom wouldn't let her talk on the phone when you called. Hey, I was there. I know. Phoebe felt like she'd let you down."

Ryan's eyes widened. "Really?" She sniffled. "You're not just saying that?"

"I'm not just saying that."

"Well . . ." She cast him an accusing look. *"You* thought I was crazy."

"I've always thought you're crazy. I *know* you're crazy."

In spite of everything Ryan had to smile. "Well, that certainly makes me feel better."

"Don't mention it." Jinx glanced down at her, cleared his throat, looked away. "So . . . you hungry or something?"

"Not really."

He nodded, started to say more, turned toward the door instead. "Well . . . see you around."

Ryan watched him go out the front door of the police station and head down the sidewalk. She took a final wipe at her eyes, then hurried after him, pulling on her jacket as she burst through the door.

"Jinx!"

He turned then, and for just the briefest moment Ryan thought he actually seemed glad to see her. She paused beside him, searching for words.

"Will you . . . tell Phoebe I said hi?"

"Like I don't have better things to do than deliver your messages." He scowled and hunched his shoulders. "Oh, and don't worry about your stupid dance —she's gonna get to go."

"You're kidding—how did she manage that?"

Jinx gave an exasperated sigh. "I told Dad to *let* her, okay?"

"Did you really?" Ryan stepped toward him, but he backed away. "Jinx, that was so sweet of you—"

"Self-defense," he said quickly. "That's all. She was crying so loud, I couldn't get any sleep." He moved away, but Ryan caught his sleeve.

"Jinx—wait."

Again he looked at her. This time she put one hand cautiously to his cheek, feeling it harden beneath her touch.

"You're going to have a scar here, aren't you?" she said quietly. "Where that bullet grazed you."

"Big deal."

"I think it's kind of sexy."

A muscle twitched in his jaw. He lowered his head, and she could swear he blushed a little.

"Oh, Jinx—" She shook her head and sighed. "That's not really what I came out here to say."

He was staring at her, getting that suspicious expression on his face, and she hurried before she lost her nerve.

"I just wanted to thank you. If you hadn't called and followed me this morning—"

"Hey"—he shrugged—"it was better than going to school—"

"No, it's for more than that. It's for everything. For always being there every time I was scared and confused and needed someone."

Jinx looked away quickly, staring at the sidewalk as if he suddenly found it intensely fascinating.

"And I just want you to know that I didn't believe a word of what Phoebe said that night," Ryan rushed on. "I mean, I know she was upset and it wasn't *true*, all those things she said—" She broke off and took a deep breath. "Was it?"

Jinx's head came up, startled.

"Right, McCauley. You should be so lucky."

He glanced away, but then his eyes came back again . . . reluctant but curious.

"So . . ." Ryan said casually, "are you going to the New Year's dance?"

"Well, yeah." Jinx shrugged. "Yeah, as soon as I decide which girl deserves the honor."

"How about me?"

He looked so taken aback that she almost laughed but managed to catch herself in time.

"Yeah, sure," he said gruffly. "How about you what?"

"I'm serious. How about me? Going with you to the dance?"

This time there was no mistaking it. As he ducked his head, a blush worked its way slowly up over his cheekbones, and Ryan wondered why she'd never realized before how irresistible it made him look.

"Well," he said, taking his time, as if considering hundreds of possibilities, "there'll be a lot of really disappointed girls . . ."

"But one really happy one."

Jinx gave a loud sigh. "Look, McCauley—"

"So?"

"So what?"

"So are you going to ask me?"

He started to grin, his head nodding slyly. "Yeah, okay. But only on one condition."

"What's that?"

"You gotta promise to wear a bag over your head."

As she took a swing at him, he caught her hand in one of his own, and they started walking.

Pawnee Public Library

About the Author

It's no secret Richie Tankersley Cusick loves to read and write scary books. Richie enjoys writing when it is rainy and gloomy outside, and likes to have a spooky soundtrack playing in the background. She writes at a desk which originally belonged to a funeral director in the 1800s and which she believes is haunted. Halloween is one of her favorite holidays. She and her husband decorate the entire house, which includes having a body laid out in state in the parlor, lifesize models of Frankenstein's monster, the figure of Death to keep watch, and a scary costume for Hannah, their dog. A neighbor recently told them that a previous owner of the house was feared by all of the neighborhood kids and no one would go to the house on Halloween.

Richie is the author of *Vampire* and *Fatal Secrets*. She and her husband, Rick, live outside Kansas City, where is currently at work on her next novel.

RICHIE TANKERSLEY CUSICK

It's the kiss of death...

VAMPIRE

When bodies are found with the mark of the vampire on their throats and Darcy Thomas receives a note saying she is "the chosen one"—it means chosen for death. Suspects surround her and it's hard to say who you can trust when the sun goes down. Can she unmask the vampire before it's too late?

Join Richie Tankersley Cusick on a journey into the terror and tension of this truly spellbinding tale.

☐ **Vampire** .... 70596-9/$3.50

POCKET
BOOKS

Simon & Schuster Mail Order Dept.
200 Old Tappan Rd., Old Tappan, N.J. 07675

Please send me the books I have checked above. I am enclosing $_____ (please add 75¢ to cover postage and handling for each order. Please add appropriate local sales tax). Send check or money order—no cash or C.O.D.'s please. Allow up to six weeks for delivery. For purchases over $10.00 you may use VISA/ MASTERCARD: card number, expiration date and customer signature must be included.

Name _____

Address _____

City _____ State/Zip _____

VISA Card No. _____ Exp. Date _____

Signature _____ 482